S0-CNQ-004

2 HOMETOWN HUNTERS
COLLECTION

The Hunt for Scarface

Lane Walker

Other books
in the Hometown Hunters Collection

The Legend of the Ghost Buck
Terror on Deadwood Lake
The Boss on Redemption Road
The Day It Rained Ducks
The Lost Deer Camp

The Hunt for Scarface
by Lane Walker
Copyright ©2014 Lane Walker

All rights reserved. This book is protected under the copyright laws of the United States of America. This book may not be copied or reprinted for commercial gain or profit.

ISBN 978-0-9853548-6-2
For Worldwide Distribution
Printed in the U.S.A.

The Hometown Hunters Collection

www.lanewalkerbooks.com

To all those who chase
their dreams and keep the faith.
All my love to my family and friends
who continue to support & inspire me.
An extra special thanks to my wife
and daughters who bring me
constant joy and happiness.
Keep hunting your dreams!

~ 1 ~

I will never forget the first time I heard HIM!

At first, my twin brother Kyle and I thought the noise was thunder, but it wasn't. We looked over toward the horizon on our farm in Nebraska and could see dark, creepy storm clouds approaching, but they weren't near enough yet to cause the loud noise we'd just heard.

Then we heard it boom again. GOBBLE! GOBBLE!

The sound made even the smallest hairs on the back of my neck stiffen, and my body turned cold. I have heard plenty of turkeys gobbling, but there was something completely different with this one, something both powerful and mysterious at the same time.

"What on earth was that, Kyle?" I asked.

At first Kyle didn't answer; he just stared.

"I don't know, Kent, but whatever it is, I hope it's heading the other way!" said Kyle.

We didn't hear that awful sound again after it began to rain. At first it was just a light drizzle. We stood in our backyard, baseball gloves in hand and decided our game of catch was over for the moment. We waited and listened. Then suddenly a thunderclap shook us back to reality. The rain changed from a lazy mist to a complete downpour. It felt like stones slamming into us as we took off running for the porch.

Thunder boomed and lightning flashed, casting an eerie glow on the entire house just as we reached the back porch. A lightning bolt zapped one of the huge oak trees in the backyard searing a massive branch that crashed to the ground. The tree always did have a mysterious quality about it. Now after the lightning strike, it looked bizarre.

In an instant the lightning had charred the bark an ugly black so that it cast a dark shadow over the backyard. I stared at it, and then Kyle grabbed me and pushed me through the door.

I looked at Kyle and grinned.

"Seems like the beginning of another adventure, what do you think?" I asked.

Unlike me, Kyle is patient. He likes to think things through and analyze every situation. But not me. I'm just the opposite. I'm extremely impulsive; I always act before I think. I was ready to investigate what that awful turkey noise was all about as soon as the storm cleared out.

I had a feeling that we were going to encounter a bird we had heard stories about all our life. Neither of us thought there was anything to them, but at this point I wasn't sure.

Right now, though, it was raining so hard I could barely make out the burnt tree through the kitchen window.

Kyle tilted his head to the side, trying to figure out all the chaos that had just happened. Little did we know that this storm was just the start of a crazy, life-changing adventure.

~ 2 ~

Kyle and I are twins, not identical but still twins. When most people think of twins, they think of two people who look exactly alike. But we don't resemble each other at all.

I have dark brown hair and Kyle is a redhead. In fact, his nickname around school is Big Red because of his height and flaming red hair.

We were born exactly thirty-seven minutes apart on a stormy spring night in Nebraska. Our mom and dad always teased us that we shook and lit up their world just like that spring thunderstorm. We definitely came into this world with a bang!

Colossal spring storms aren't uncommon in Nebraska, but the day we were born was one of the worst on record. It was so bad the hospital's electricity went out and they had to run a generator so there was enough light for the doctors to deliver us.

Thunder and lightning are what we are. I'm the loud, boisterous one, and Kyle is quiet; but when he talks, he's wise and people listen, including me. We're best friends most of the time. Living with a twin brother is no easy task, especially one like me.

My favorite sport is football, and Kyle loves basketball although we play both. I'm the quarterback of our football team. As a quarterback, I love throwing touchdown passes especially to my favorite receiver, #9. Kyle wore #9, of course.

Kyle is the best basketball player in the entire school, even though we're only freshmen. Coaches talk about starting Kyle on the varsity as a sophomore.

During most of our basketball games, I'd just pass him the ball and watch him do his thing. There isn't another player smoother than #35 Kyle Morris. When #35 has the ball, the entire gym waits for something great to happen.

Nevertheless, there are some things we don't

have in common. For instance, Kyle doesn't really care for pets, but animals always make me smile. I remember when we were young and Mom read us *Old Yeller* by Fred Gipson. I cried and cried at the end. I guess the Lord just made me an animal lover.

My favorite pet is my dog, Rambo. He's a mutt by most people's standards but not to me. He's my friend and I have spent hours playing with him and teaching him. We rescued Rambo from our local pet shelter, and I loved the dog the instant I saw him.

Even with those minor differences, Kyle and I usually complement each other. I'd get the peanut butter; he'd get the jelly. He'd get the milk; I'd get the cookies.

Besides sports, there's another love we both share—hunting. Ever since we were old enough to hold a bow or a gun, we enjoyed being in the woods. Dad taught us at a young age to respect animals and the weapons we were using. We have great parents. Our mom is a kindergarten teacher, and our dad manages the local hardware store.

Our dad holds a special spot in our hearts—he's our hero. When Dad graduated from high school, he entered the Marines. He served four years and traveled to several countries. Once his enlisted time was up, he returned home to work at Bellsville Hardware.

The Morris family has a long line of servicemen and servicewomen dating back to the Civil War. Our dad always told us there is no bigger earthly honor than to serve and risk your life protecting our country.

My great-grandpa was an important general in World War I. We never had a chance to meet him because he was killed during the war, but Dad always told us stories of his bravery and heroism during the toughest parts of battle. While we're too young to enlist, both Kyle and I plan to be Navy Seals or Army Rangers after high school.

Our dad loves to hunt. It's something important to him and something he enjoys, so it became important to us as well. In fact, Dad taught us how to hunt deer and turkey at a young age. Kyle's favorite is deer while mine is turkey.

Nothing gets my blood pumping faster than those old thunder chickens. Even playing sports doesn't provide the same adrenaline rush I get when I go turkey hunting. There is nothing better than the wet smell of spring in the woods and the loud gobble of a lovelorn tom turkey.

Even though I'm only 14, I'd already taken a number of jakes and toms. Every hunting season, Kyle and I added more trophies to our parents' wall. We were starting to think we were getting good at this hunting thing, as if we were a couple young experts conquering the wild woods of Nebraska. We had that idea until we met, or should I say heard, HIM the day of the storm.

If this turkey was the one of our town's legend, there was nothing ordinary about him. It's said that his gobble was so loud and deep that it made grown men tremble.

Only a handful of people had ever seen the bird. He was so big that several locals had mistaken him for a small deer. He supposedly had the reddish, most fearsome head anyone in

Nebraska had ever seen, if you ever got close enough to get a glimpse. Most of the time, people only heard him. His gobble was unmistakable—a mix between an old chainsaw and a blaring horn on a semi-truck. When he let loose, the whole woods stopped and listened.

This turkey was like no other He had a secret—he always seemed to be able to disappear without a trace.

Bellsville was known for its rich American history. But now it was about to be known for something else— the birthplace of a turkey we later named Scarface.

~ 3 ~

Bellsville is nestled about forty miles outside of Omaha along the Platte River. It's a quaint town of farmers and factory workers. Like most towns in the Midwest, the community revolves around the local high school. Every Friday night during football season, the entire town shuts down and packs the high school football field.

We don't have a ton of factories, but there are a couple that provide jobs for most of the town. One is Titus Trailers, a well-known trailer manufacturing company. The owner and CEO, Tom Titus, is a local celebrity.

Besides having a multi-million dollar business, Mr. Titus donated a lot of money to our high school football team. In fact, the stadium is named Titus Stadium, reflecting his generosity.

It's a gorgeous stadium, complete with a huge

heated press box, and the field has the best artificial turf that money can buy. All this was courtesy of Mr. Titus, who was well-known long before becoming a business tycoon.

He'd been a football star at Bellsville High School decades ago. Not only was he the star quarterback, but he helped take the Bellsville Bobcats to their only state championship game.

With eight seconds on the clock, the score was 23-21 with the Central Omaha Bucks leading the Bobcats. The Bobcats were on the Bucks' twenty-yard line, about to score the game-winning touchdown. There was time for one last play, one that would forever haunt a small, football-crazy town.

It was up to the golden boy, the quarterback, all-stater Tom Titus to do what he had done so many times before. It was time for him to be the savior of Bellsville. He avoided a sack, ran to his left and heaved a throw into the end zone to his best friend and star wide receiver, Mike Morris, who eventually became my dad.

The ball floated through the air slowly as the

crowd rose to its feet. Dad jumped between two defenders and caught the ball. Out of bounds! Game over. Bellsville was the Nebraska state runner-up, not state champion.

Tom always blamed Dad for stepping out of bounds. Even though everyone knew it was a bad throw, deep down he resented my dad for Bellsville losing that game.

After high school, Dad headed into the military and Tom went to business school. One thing about Tom, he had to be the best. The spotlight always had to shine on him and only him. Dad always knew that but had managed to see the good in Tom and ignore the rest.

They had grown up together and were best friends from the third grade until that final game in high school. Afterwards they became bitter enemies. One thing that didn't help their friendship was Dad's wedding. After returning home from the Marines, he fell in love with and married my mom, Tom's only sister, making him my uncle.

The final straw came about five years ago

when Uncle Tom bought two acres that bordered our property. The land wasn't worth much and had been for sale for years. It was basically a small woodlot with some high grass near the front toward the road. Dad had looked at buying it at one point, but the real estate company wanted too much money.

Money was not an option for Uncle Tom. He bought the land with cash. After he purchased it, he put up a huge billboard advertising one of his several car dealerships. The sign was lit up with a smiling picture of Uncle Tom. Many townspeople would joke that it was one of the only times they had ever seen Tom Titus smile. Dad had to look at that sign every day. We all knew that Uncle Tom had done that on purpose, just to taunt Dad.

Uncle Tom had a son and a daughter. My cousin, Tom Jr., is the same age as Kyle and me. Around town, everyone knows him as T.J. Even though we're the same age, we aren't close to T.J. In fact, we seldom ever talk to him and think he's a spoiled brat.

T.J. is jealous of Kyle and me. He always had

big dreams of being a high school quarterback like his dad. But everyone in Bellsville knew I earned the position this year. That always bothers T.J., but I think it bothers his dad the most.

The Titus family wasn't the only family with strong roots in Bellsville. Our family lived on a homestead that had been in my dad's family for more than two hundred years. My dad had grown up on the family farm, which was about a half mile from our house. The original Morris farm consisted of four hundred eighty acres, mostly farm fields, but there were also several large woodlots. Several years ago, my grandpa had retired from farming and divided his land. He sold over half the farm and gave my dad and dad's sister, Aunt Michele, each some acreage. They both built houses on Hall Road just outside Bellsville's city limits.

Kyle and I love to spend time in and around the woods on our family's properties. Aunt Michelle and her husband, Anderson, have three daughters. They are a lot younger than we are, so we get free reign to hunt and play in the woods as much as we want.

We have always tried to take full advantage of the family farm, spending as much time outside as we can, exploring every inch of the property. Lately, however, it was getting tougher and tougher with all the sports practices. Football started every August. After football we went right into basketball and when that was over, our spring was spent playing baseball.

Soon, however, our days were going to be taken up with something more than just sports.

~ 4 ~

After the lightning storm had passed and the rain had quit, Kyle and I grabbed our camouflage and turkey vests. Once we had on all our gear, we took off toward a big bean field on the back of our property. It was a great spot to hunt turkeys. The field was isolated away from any roads and surrounded by big trees. Behind the field was the river, which added extra privacy for the birds.

Turkeys love to roost in the nearby trees and fly down to munch on leftover soybeans. We had hunted and killed many big toms in this area and knew that was where that awful gobble had probably come from.

Even though the storm had passed, there was some thunder off in the distance toward town. The dark, gray clouds still rolled over our heads, and the wind started to pick up slightly.

Just before we reached the edge of the woods that connected with the bean field, I stopped.

"Why are you stopping?" Kyle whispered. I started scanning the timber and undergrowth. We were still about fifty yards from the bean field.

Suddenly, I caught movement out of the corner of my eye. I turned to see three birds running away from us toward the deep woods. I quickly pulled up my gun.

"Hens! Don't shoot," yelled Kyle.

That's when we saw HIM for the first time. A huge tom turkey took off from behind a log about twenty feet away. I had enough time to see his big red head and pulled up to fire. I shot and the bird fell.

"I got him!" I shouted back to Kyle.

I started toward the bird. When I was within about ten feet, he jumped up. What I saw next both terrified me and sent a wave of excitement through my body like I never experienced before.

The turkey was so massive, his beard dragged the ground. He quickly jumped up on the log. I fumbled around with the gun to put in another shell, but I couldn't get the gun open. The gobbler managed to stop as he ran down the log. He turned and stared right at me and let out the most horrifying gobble, the same sound Kyle and I had heard right before the storm.

Up close, the gobbler looked even more fierce. Its call echoed through the woods and was louder than any thunder I had ever heard.

My single-shot was jammed.

As the turkey turned to run away, I noticed a long vertical cut above his right eye. It seemed to be about three inches from the top of his head and ran all the way down his cheek.

I had only nicked the bird with my shot. Maybe one pellet had hit him. I think I might have scraped him. It wasn't a kill shot, but it was something that old bird would remember for a long time. I watched in disbelief as the huge turkey ran out of sight.

"Did you get him?" Kyle asked, as he caught up with me.

"No, I might have skimmed him but didn't hurt him at all," I said sadly.

"Kent, I have never seen a bird that big. His beard was at least fifteen inches long!"

"I know. Thanks for reminding me. I think we just saw what a world record turkey looks like, brother. I can't believe this stupid old gun jammed just when I needed it the most."

With that, I took the gun and slammed it against a nearby tree. The gun popped open, the empty shell fell out, and it broke in two.

Despite my missing the bird, this turkey was about to change everything in the Morris house. The town's legend was confirmed to be real that day.

I made up my mind. I wouldn't settle for any other bird, only my new enemy, Scarface, would do.

~ 5 ~

I was so mad!

I had never missed a turkey before. Here I had a chance at the biggest turkey I'd ever seen, and I screwed it up. Not only that, now the .16 gauge was broken.

I was not looking forward to telling my dad. That gun had been in our family for years. It was a wedding gift to my dad from my grandpa. I guess he thought it was a good gift for someone marrying his only daughter.

Personally I hated that old gun and would have sold it in a second for a new shotgun, one that wouldn't jam.

"You know you shouldn't have slammed the gun," Kyle finally said as we walked into the backyard.

"Don't you think I know that now? But it's a

stupid gun anyway. It's old, rusty, and only has one shot. We need one of those new, fancy pump shotguns, like the one that Dad sells at the hardware store," I said.

"We've killed lots of birds with that gun. Dad killed his first turkey with it. I think Grandpa even used that gun. Besides it wasn't the gun that caused you to miss," said Kyle.

I just looked at him. Of course it wasn't the gun. I knew that, but it felt better if I could find something else to blame it on. The truth was I had hurried and taken a bad shot. I should have just let the turkey go.

"That is one gutsy bird! To stop and gobble at me after I had just had him in my crosshairs. I've never seen or heard anything like that before," I said to Kyle.

Kyle stopped and stared off toward the woods. He liked to think things out while I liked to blurt out the first thing on my mind. However, when he did speak, I always listened. Kyle was wise for a fifteen-year-old.

"There's something about that bird. I don't

know what it is yet, but I felt something back there. Something exciting," said Kyle.

Weird, I felt the same way. There was definitely something unique about that old gobbler. At first, I couldn't put my finger on it. The only thing I could focus on was that I had missed.

That bird was going to take us to a special place, a place where most people perhaps wouldn't want to go.

~ 6 ~

That night Dad got home late from work. When he did arrive, we were happy to see him. After telling him our turkey hunting story, he just started to laugh.

"Did Grandpa tell you that story?" Dad asked.

Kyle and I looked at each other. We hadn't told anyone about our turkey hunt.

"No, Dad, it happened just like that," I said.

He looked at Kyle; between the two of us, it was much easier for him to believe Kyle than me. I had a history of telling some stories and exaggerating.

"Is he serious?" Dad asked.

Kyle nodded. Dad took a deep breath.

"Boys, come out to the barn with me for a second. There is something there I want to show you," said Dad.

With that, we all headed out to the barn. My mind was racing as we walked in. Dad was usually a low-key person, but I could see that something inside him was burning. What could he have to show us?

He retrieved an old crate hidden behind a bunch of rusty tractor parts and set it on his wooden workbench. He pulled something out and set it down in front of us.

"Wow! That's a huge beard!" I shouted.

In front of us was a ten-inch super thick beard that looked almost like a horse's tail. Kyle examined the beard like a surgeon.

"Dad, why is it unevenly cut at the top?" Kyle asked.

He was right. I didn't notice it at first, but the beard looked almost like it was chopped.

Dad said, "I missed a huge turkey but managed to shoot a piece of his beard off. That was years ago in the same field where you boys shot at your big bird. My bird did the same thing. I rolled him right over, and he jumped up and ran toward the woods. I never saw him again."

Dad added, "This was a once-in-a-lifetime turkey. I have never seen another bird even close in size. Besides having a good story, this part of his beard is the only evidence I have of that turkey."

"Why did you only shoot once? Why didn't you finish the bird off when you had a chance?" I asked.

Dad looked down and then out the window. His response surprised me and added a completely new element to the events of the day. A simple three-word sentence caused my mind to race. The words echoed in my mind.

"The gun jammed."

At first, I was angry. I wondered, if the same gun had jammed on my father so many years ago, why in the world would he have us use it? Didn't he want us to get a turkey?

We went inside to have dinner. Mom cooked venison steaks with a side of asparagus. She also baked one of our favorite things—we called it "Kyle Bread" because Kyle loved it and often tried to eat the whole pan himself. Mom also made homemade bread sticks and smothered them in cheese. For dessert, she cut us each pieces of her famous blackberry pie.

During dinner, we were all quiet.

"Wow, look what happened to that old oak tree. It's strange that lightning hit that particular one, even though there are much bigger ones all around," Dad said.

Kyle and I looked at each other. That wasn't the strangest thing that had happened or would happen in the days to come.

~ 7 ~

I woke up for school early that Monday. I was restless and couldn't sleep. I still hadn't told my dad about breaking that old single-shot. I knew he was going to be mad, so I was trying to avoid the entire situation.

I hid the two pieces of the gun under my bed, but knew it was only a matter of time before I would have to tell him.

The sun was just starting to come up. Kyle was still sleeping; I can always tell because he snores. I looked out the window toward the back of our property where we had encountered the turkey.

Suddenly, something caught my eye. At first, I thought it was my dog, Rambo. But that theory went up in smoke when I heard him barking over by the barn. I squinted as the sun peeked over the horizon and was right in my eyes. That old tree, the one that had been hit by lightning, looked eerie. The orange and red of the rising sun gave it a unique white glow. For a second it looked like a huge hand was up in it, but the rising sun blinded me, ending my view of the tree.

"Hey," Kyle grunted.

"What's your problem?" I asked.

"The sun is so bright it hurts my eyes."

He yawned and glanced out the window. He squinted to look at the tree and turned to me. Kyle could tell by the look on my face that something was going on.

We didn't have much time to think about it before the morning silence was broken by the loud distant gobble of a turkey.

At first, I felt excited, but it didn't last.

"It's not him, it's not the turkey from yesterday," I said disappointedly.

"How do you know?"

"There's no mistaking his gobble. I knew that it wasn't him. It couldn't be."

His gobble could almost shake the picture

frames on our wall. It was a gobbler but not the one I was interested in.

That morning we couldn't get to school fast enough. I don't like riding the school bus. Not only are we the first ones on, but we have to sit near our cousin T.J. and listen to him talk about himself. Today would be no different.

I listened as T.J. was telling all the elementary kids about his trips to Africa and about all his video games. He always had the best and most expensive things, and he liked to make sure everyone knew it.

I closed my eyes, but all I could see was that big old gobbler sitting on that dead log gobbling at me. It kept running through my mind.

I drifted off to sleep, only to wake up to the sound of the screeching brakes from our bus. We had finally arrived. Kyle and I got off the bus and headed for our math class. I didn't mind math, but on the likeability scale it couldn't match P.E. or lunch.

The day seemed to drag on. We ate lunch and headed to Mr. Potter's history class.

"Good afternoon, class. Today we are going to start an important project. We are going to look at our local history . . . a history that is unique and important to America . . . a history that helped form the great state of Nebraska as we know it!"

Mr. Potter always had a flare for the dramatic.

History often intrigued me, especially our local history. Mr. Potter went on to tell us that in 1803 the United States purchased the Louisiana Territory from France for fifteen million dollars. Everyone in class gasped when he said how much it cost—everyone but one person.

"My dad could buy that," T.J. declared in a loud voice.

Everyone turned and glared at him.

"Class, each one of you will have to do a report about the history of Bellsville," announced Mr. Potter, ignoring T.J.

For the rest of the hour, Mr. Potter went on to describe how wild Nebraska was. He mentioned the Kansas-Nebraska Act, stagecoaches, and the Pony Express, which was a famous mail service where riders risked life and limb to get mail to the trailblazers heading west. Then he started talking about fur trading camps and how all the hunters and Native Americans would set up there and trade. Bellsville was also a popular place among pioneers because it was located on the Platte River. We learned that Platte is from the French word for "flat."

I was hooked. I bet there were huge deer, beaver, and turkeys at those camps. I started to doodle on my paper and draw big bucks and huge turkeys. My mind was racing. I was off in my own world when Kyle bumped my arm.

"Isn't that near our farm?" Kyle whispered.

I looked up and noticed that Mr. Potter had gotten out an old map with a bunch of fur trading posts on it. I squinted to try to make out the names and locations of the camps.

Just then, the bell rang, and the map was put away.

~ 8 ~

"Mr. Potter, can I borrow that map?" I asked him on my way out.

"I was really intrigued by the whole Nebraska history lesson," I said, hoping that would help me get the map.

"That's good to know, Mr. Morris. You can borrow my map but keep in mind it's very old and very special. There aren't many of these maps out there. Please take good care of it."

The map was fragile and old. It had a hard, dry feeling and a unique, musty smell. It reminded me of a mix between bathroom cleaner and a hospital. The map had a strange presence about it. There was just something that made it special.

As I was leaving, Mr. Potter had one last thing to say.

"Kent, you never know what treasures you can find when you're exploring history."

I smiled, not really knowing what he meant, but it sounded somewhat cool. As I went to my locker, I could feel someone following me. I turned. To my surprise, it was T.J.

"What's so special about that old map?" he asked.

I stopped. I had to be careful. I didn't want to let him know that the map looked like our property had once been an amazing fur trading post full of life, people, and wild animals.

Just as I was about to say something, Kyle walked up.

"Hey, I hope you got that map. It will definitely help us write our history paper for Mr. Potter's class. I think it'll be interesting to see how small Bellsville used to be," said Kyle.

I looked at him with a smile.

"That's stupid, I would just have my dad call someone in the mayor's office and make them tell us. You don't need an old map to know that my dad helped build this town. We pretty much own half of it anyway," said T.J. who stalked off shaking his head.

"Thanks, Kyle, you saved me once again," I said.

I could tell that Kyle had something on his mind. The right side of his lip started to twitch, so I knew he was excited about something.

"I saw it too. It looks like the back of our property was part of that old trading post," Kyle whispered.

I needed to confirm my initial thought, so Kyle and I ducked into an empty classroom. The room is used for art class, so there was an overwhelming smell of old paints and construction paper.

I quickly wiped off one of the bigger tables and pulled out the mysterious map. As I unfolded it, it rustled like it was trying to tell us something.

The first thing I noticed was the writing. It wasn't English, I was sure of that.

"It looks like it's written in French," said Kyle.

I nodded although I hadn't taken the language.

The first thing we looked for was the Platte River. I knew once we found that we could pinpoint our house. A very distinctive curve ran along the back of our family's homestead. It was one of my favorite spots on the entire property.

Even though the map was faded, we had no trouble finding the river. We saw what we thought was Omaha and followed the river toward Bellsville.

"There!" I said excitedly. "Kyle, there's the fort!"

Sure enough, right where the river curved, written in big letters were the words "Forte de Bellsville." The fort looked big on the map, covering both sides of the river. On our side of the river, it looked like it was the main encampment and docking area.

I remember Mr. Potter telling us how fur traders used the river as a main travel route connecting fur trading posts. Sure enough, there was a sketch of a small dock for the fort.

Suddenly, Kyle grabbed my arm.

"Look!" he said, pointing to the outside of the

fort, which was located on our land. There were two symbols—a huge set of antlers and a picture of a huge turkey. We knew what those symbols meant. It identified where the hunters and fur traders camped and traded.

And it was on our side of the river, right on our property!

~ 9 ~

I snuck over to my locker and hid the map between my library book and math textbook. I quickly shut my locker and heard it click as the lock latched. I joined Kyle and we headed down to our fifth hour P.E. class.

In P.E. we were doing a unit on volleyball, but I was having trouble concentrating. I was day-dreaming about early hunters with their long muskets and Native Americans chasing down monster bucks with their traditional wooden bows.

Suddenly, Kyle elbowed me, bringing me back to reality.

"Ouch, what do you want?" I asked.

He cupped his hand to his ear, motioning me to listen.

"Do you hear it?" he asked.

The gym was loud. I heard all kinds of conversations. There was a group of girls talking about their hair and make-up. Another group of kids were complaining about all the homework from Mr. Fitz's algebra class.

Just as I was turning to ask Kyle what he was talking about, I heard it. As loud as the gym was, I noticed it.

There was something strange—T.J. wasn't around bragging about himself. I looked at Kyle and took off through the gym door toward my locker. Just as I turned the corner, I saw T.J. and he saw me.

I ran toward him. He shut my locker, turned to run, and tripped over his backpack. I jumped on him and pinned him to the ground.

"Give it to me!"

At first, he acted surprised, but I tightened my grip. He finally broke free and got to his feet. He reached in his back pocket, and pulled out the old brown map that Mr. Potter had let me borrow.

"What are you doing with *my* map?" I demanded.

He turned his head, not even able to look me in the eye. What a coward! I grabbed one side of the map, but T.J. ripped the other half away. Brown crusty flakes exploded on the hallway floor.

I shook my head. I couldn't believe that he had stolen the map and now part of it was in pieces. I jumped up and saw the back of his back-pack as he ran down the hall toward the office. My Aunt Carol, T.J.'s mom, was the principal's secretary. I knew where he was going—he was going to hide behind his mommy.

I looked back at Kyle.

"I can't stand T.J.!" I cried.

Not only did we lose half the map, now I had to figure out a way to tell Mr. Potter that it was partially ruined.

I don't know what made me madder—knowing that T.J. broke into my locker or having him tear the map in two.

"He knows something's going on," Kyle finally said.

My problems were about to get worse, much

worse. I quickly unraveled the piece of the map. It was the only thing I had left. I held it up to the light in the hallway. I knew before I even looked that we had the wrong half of the map. Our half showed the other side of the river. T.J. still had our piece of the map.

I was so tired of T.J. I didn't care if he was family. As far as I was concerned, he was just a big problem.

But I didn't have time to worry about him now. Kyle and I had a new mission.

- 10 -

For some strange reason, T.J. didn't ride the bus home from school that day. It was probably better that way, I thought.

I wanted to embarrass him. I had all kinds of devious plans of how I was going to tease him on the bus and get everyone to laugh at him.

I was much bigger, more athletic, and feared in our school. T.J. knew it and, more importantly, I knew it.

"Calm down," Kyle said.

I looked at him. He could see the rage in my eyes.

"How can you always be so calm, so under control? You can't let someone steal from us, Kyle!"

"Kent, we saw the map. Even though T.J. has it, we know where the fort was. It's on our property, not his. We don't even know if the map is accurate," Kyle said.

He added, "And you know T.J. I'm not making excuses for him, but most of it is not his fault."

Kyle always knew what to say to me and his last sentence hit me hard. I did know about Uncle Tom and the way he treated T.J.

My real issues were more with Uncle Tom. They didn't have anything to do with T.J.

During the bus ride home, I made a decision. I turned to Kyle and said with a grin, "We need to find this fort. We can't tell anyone what we're doing. What if there's still treasure hidden there?"

"I'm sure we aren't the first ones to ever explore the old fort," Kyle said.

Maybe they weren't even looking in the right spot. Mr. Potter said the map had been found at an old estate sale. He added that not too many people had seen it before.

I couldn't help but think about all the details on the map. I tried to remember every little thing I had seen before T.J. ripped it.

A red X. A big red X. I saw one on it, and that

had to mean one thing—treasure! There's always treasure hidden under an X on a map.

As soon as we got off the bus, we ran to our room. We have a big desk there, and Kyle grabbed a sheet of paper. We slowly started to draw what we remembered of the other half of the map.

We went back and forth over a couple things, but overall we both had a good mental picture of the missing map piece. We knew that the fort was located near a distinct bend in the river. There were only two spots where the river turned so drastically. One was near the western border of our property. We were both familiar with the spot. It was a great place to catch small bass and shoot ducks in the fall. Kyle and I had fished and explored there for years.

"I don't remember seeing anything that resembled an old fort or any type of encampment near Gulliver's Hole," Kyle said.

He was right. There were smaller oak trees and a couple birch trees that bordered the creek, but that was all.

The other bend in the river held more mystery. We had a basic idea of where it was, but it was a place we didn't explore much. For one reason, it always felt spooky when we went there.

In order to get back to the second bend, we would have to walk through a part of the woods that we usually avoided. We had nicknamed the spot the Dungeon because it was so thick and dark. We never saw any animals or found tracks in this area. It was full of briars and sharp stickers.

"That's it! I have no doubt that's where the encampment was. We haven't spent much time there, and not many people have ventured into that part of the woods," said Kyle.

He was right. He had to be. Now we had a good idea of where to start looking, but another major problem surfaced. If we could get back to the spot, through the Dungeon, how would we find any proof of the old fort?

We looked at each other. My mind started to wander. I pictured Kyle and me digging for forty years looking for something, anything to reinforce in our minds that we were looking in the right spot. We would both have long gray beards and be hobbling around from hole to hole, hoping and praying for some artifact that would prove to everyone we had found the old fort.

My daydream was broken when I caught a glimpse of the look on Kyle's face. I knew that look; it was a look of genius! Whenever he had that stare, something marvelous was about to happen.

Last year our basketball team was undefeated heading into our last game of the season against our crosstown rival, Marsh Ridge. That was the last time I saw that stare, a champion's stare.

We were down one with ten seconds left in the game. Our school hadn't beaten Marsh Ridge in the past five years. Our coach called a timeout and drew a play that had me making the last shot and using Kyle as a decoy. Just before we broke the huddle, I looked at my brother, and Kyle was standing there with that look!

"Coach, let Kyle take the last shot. I know he'll make it!" I said.

He looked at me and looked at Kyle.

Kyle nodded.

"Okay," said Coach Winkle.

We went out, and I set a pick for Kyle. He dribbled left, crossed over, and pulled up at the free throw line. At the buzzer, the only sound I heard was the swishing of the net as Kyle's shot found the basket.

Our whole school rushed the floor and mobbed us. They picked up Kyle, carrying him around the gym on their shoulders.

I knew the look. I liked it. When I saw it, I new something magical was going to happen.

I was right!

~ 11 ~

Our birthday was only a week away.

The only gift I wanted was a new shotgun, and I had been begging Dad the entire year. I was sick of that old hand-me-down .16-gauge. I still had nightmares about missing that huge turkey. In my mind, the main reason for the miss was the gun.

I didn't know much about the old single-shot. What I did know, I didn't like. The hammer cocked hard. I had to use both hands and all my might to cock it.

The trigger always stuck, making it really hard to pull. The barrel had a light coating of rust. Now the stock was broken, but that was my fault.

Kyle smiled. I knew he had an idea.

"What's on your mind?" I asked.

"I know what we need to get for our birthday," he said.

"Yeah, I know too. A new shotgun. I never plan on missing another long beard again," I said.

Kyle shook his head.

"Kyle, we need a new gun bad! What do *you* think we should get for our birthday?"

"A metal detector," Kyle said.

What a genius! I had never thought of that. What a perfect idea! If we got a metal detector, we really could explore the area around the old fort. We might even find some artifacts or, better yet, the missing treasure.

This history project was starting to consume both of us. Not only did I want to get an A on the report, I wanted to explore our property's history.

There was one big problem though. I had my heart set on a new shotgun. In my mind, we already had it. I couldn't see myself using that old single-shot ever again.

I started to think about it and realized that Kyle was right; it was our only hope. If we really intended on finding the old fort, we would need a metal detector. We didn't have any money to get one, so our only hope was to ask for one for our birthday. One nice thing about being twins, Mom and Dad tried to get us one big present we could share. Last year, it was a new hunting tent for turkey season. Kyle shot a big gobbler from the tent last spring.

On the other hand, my mind still kept racing about that huge turkey I think I had nicked. The thunder gobbler ran off scarred but alive. I don't know if I even hit him or if he actually cut his head on a branch.

Whatever the case, he was huge and still alive! This year my turkey hunting plans were simple— find Scarface! Even more than that, I wanted to find out his secret. Where did he hide? Where did he go? How did he always seem to disappear without a trace?

I made plans for killing that big bird. However, my original scheme had included a brand new shotgun. My desire to hunt that turkey still burned inside, but I also really wanted to find the fort.

One thing was obvious. This spring I was going to be an explorer. Whether chasing old

Scarface or digging for artifacts, I was going to find something valuable this year.

Kyle was right. Asking for a new metal detector was our only hope of finding the fort.

~ 12 ~

When we told Dad about our birthday request for the metal detector, he was a bit surprised.

"I thought the only thing you wanted was that fancy camouflage shotgun from the hardware store," he said.

I stopped. I was trying to think of a way to explain it to him without giving away our treasure-hunting plan.

"I don't mind that old gun," I said, lying through my teeth.

"Really?" Dad questioned.

I have never been a good liar.

"Dad, we've been watching a lot of treasure hunting shows on T.V., and we have an important history project for Mr. Potter's class," Kyle chimed in.

Thank you, Kyle! He always knew the right

thing to say. He was telling the truth, kind of. I tried not to make eye contact with Dad.

"What about that old .16-gauge? I thought you were tired of that gun. Didn't you tell me, Kent, how much you hated that old gun?" Dad said.

I did. Last week after missing that turkey, I remembered complaining to Dad about the gun. I did hate that gun, and not only because I missed Scarface. Unlike many of the modern shotguns, I still had to cock the hammer.

Instead of a beautiful camouflage covering, our old single-shot was a mix of rust and black paint. What's to love about that old single-shot? I couldn't see why everyone was making such a big fuss about the old gun. I never understood why my dad even kept that gun.

"I don't like it, but it'll work. Maybe next year we can get a new gun," I quickly said.

Dad looked out the window toward the back-field. There were a couple of deer milling around in the clover field.

"Speaking of that gun, where is it? I haven't seen it lately," said Dad.

Those were the words I had been trying to hide from all week.

"Kent, go grab that gun and let's take a look at it," Dad said.

I looked at Kyle, and he quickly turned away. He knew what was about to happen. He wasn't going to bail me out of this one.

"Go get the gun!" Dad repeated. He wasn't smiling anymore.

A million thoughts ripped through my mind. I was trying to think of a way to talk myself out of this situation. I felt like I was on one of those game shows and a million people were watching me, waiting for me to make a mistake.

I couldn't think of any excuse. I got up and headed to our bedroom. As soon as I opened our bedroom door, my stomach started to hurt. I crawled under my bed. I reached to the far back corner and slowly pulled both pieces of the gun out. I had run out of time. I now was about to take my punishment.

My head hung low as I walked out to the living room. Dad just stared as I laid the broken

53

pieces on the coffee table. I kept waiting for him to yell. I actually hoped he would. I thought it would be over quicker if he just yelled and let me throw that gun away.

He didn't yell. In fact, he didn't say anything. My mind raced. What's he doing? Why isn't he yelling?

I started to get even more worried. My stomach felt like a balloon about ready to burst. What happened next was worse than I ever imagined.

My dad started to cry.

~ 13 ~

In that moment, I don't think I ever felt so bad. Most of the time I'd get emotional or upset was when we lost a basketball or football game.

This was different. I had lost games and even gotten into arguments with Kyle but had never felt so low. The worst part was, I still didn't know what all the fuss was.

I mean we're talking about an old antique—a gun that was far past its prime. The trigger always jammed, there was rust on the barrel, and the sight was a little copper BB glued on the tip of the barrel.

I didn't know why my dad was so hurt, but I knew he was. Seeing him disappointed in me was worse than any type of punishment he could ever give me. Kyle put his arm around Dad. I slowly inched closer and sat next to him.

"Dad, I'm so sorry. I didn't realize how much that old, grungy gun meant to you," I said.

Dad sat up and wiped his face.

"You have no clue about this old gun."

He was right. All I knew was that Grandpa had given it to Dad when he and Mom had gotten married.

"The only thing you care about is that fancy, new shotgun," Dad said.

He was right. I would have traded that old shotgun for any new gun on the spot.

"You know, boys, newer isn't always better. I know this gun has some rust. Sometimes it's loud and hard to cock the hammer. I get all that, but you're really missing out on something much bigger. This gun has an amazing history, one that you both need to learn," Dad said.

Ouch! His words cut like a knife. Over the past couple weeks, Kyle and I had been crazy about history. And now we had something historic sitting under my bed the whole time.

It was hard to describe how I felt at that minute. I remember watching Mom cut into a warm loaf of homemade bread and the knife easily sliced through it. That was how I felt, but instead of being the knife, I was the bread, like someone just sliced me open.

"I had no idea," I quickly said.

Dad just kept examining the gun, looking it over. The way he was looking at it caught my attention. He had a certain gleam in his eye. I knew there was something he wasn't telling us.

Kyle finally spoke up. "Dad, I'd love to learn more about the history of this gun."

That Kyle! It always seems like he knows the right thing to say.

"You will. In fact, you're going to learn first hand," Dad said.

He got up and grabbed the keys to his truck. He looked at both of us with a renewed sense of pride.

"Get in the truck, boys. We're going to see your Grandpa. I'm sure he would love to tell the history of this old .16-gauge," Dad said.

The truck was silent as we rode the couple of miles to Grandpa's house. I was ashamed to tell

Grandpa how I'd broken the gun in my anger. I didn't know what I was going to say, but I knew I was going to have to tell him something. I couldn't tell him how much I hated that old gun. Maybe I could tell him how that old gun failed me when I needed it the most. Grandpa was a hunter. Maybe he'd sympathize with me about missing that huge turkey. He might understand why I threw the gun down.

I kept thinking of how I would start the conversation and slowly work into the fact that I had busted the gun.

As we pulled in, it was clear I wouldn't have to think of a way to tell him. There was a new problem. I recognized the brand new fancy sports car as soon as we pulled in.

Uncle Tom and T.J. were already there. They had stopped by for a visit.

~ 14 ~

Dad and Uncle Tom exchanged dangerous glares. As we got closer to Grandpa, I had a feeling that something bad was about to happen.

"You boys run along inside and give your grandma a kiss," Grandpa quickly said.

For a second, I thought I was off the hook. I started to walk up the squeaky steps toward the front door.

"The boys need to stay. Kent has something to show you," Dad said.

Dad pulled out the gun case and slowly unzipped it.

Uncle Tom snickered.

"That old thing. I'm surprised it has lasted this long. Why don't you just buy them a new one? Quit being cheap. All you got to do is save up all your paychecks for a month, and you could buy a new one," Tom said with a devilish grin. Then he added with sarcasm, "I would be more than happy to let my nephews borrow one of T.J.'s, he has so many."

What a jerk! Grandpa just sat there staring. The gleam in his eye had disappeared. His face slowly started to change, taking on a more serious look.

The situation was starting to get tense. For a second I thought Dad was going to walk over and punch Uncle Tom in the face. I gotta admit I wanted him to. Dad didn't take to kindly to Uncle Tom's smart remarks and neither did I.

"Tom, I think you and T.J. need to get running along," Grandpa said sternly. He had a look in his eye, a look that made even the great Tom Titus listen.

The next sound we heard was the roaring of Uncle Tom's BMW. A large cloud of dust rolled off the old dirt road as the convertible ripped out of Grandpa's driveway.

I was trying to prepare something to say to Grandpa. It was only a ten-minute drive across town to Grandpa's house, so I hadn't had much time to prepare.

"I'm sorry," I finally muttered.

I didn't really mean it. I mean I was sorry because it hurt my dad and grandpa's feelings. I still didn't see the big deal everyone was making about this old gun.

"Boys, have a seat. I think it's time I educate you both on a little family history," Grandpa said. "This gun is one of kind. There isn't another one like it on the planet. Sure, there are many single-shot .16-gauge shotguns. But there isn't another one quite like this one on the entire earth!"

Now he had our attention.

"Why? Is it expensive? Is it worth a lot of money?" I asked.

"Nope, it's not a fancy antique or anything like that. In fact, in this condition, there isn't really any monetary value at all in the gun."

"Grandpa, I noticed there are small slash marks on the forearm of the gun. Why are they there?" Kyle asked.

Until Kyle had asked that question, I had

never noticed that there were twelve small vertical slashes, almost like someone had carved them with a small jackknife. I always thought they were just wear and tear on the gun.

"Each of those marks is a memory, part of our family tree. I can tell you the story of all twelve," Grandpa said.

He first told us how his grandfather had hunted and trapped for six months to buy the gun. He went on to say that each of the slashes signified something important in our family history. Grandpa told us about a huge turkey he had shot. That was the tenth mark. The eleventh mark was the last time Grandpa went squirrel hunting with his dad. Kyle and I were mesmerized by all the stories and history of that old gun.

"Grandpa, you stopped at eleven. What was twelve? What caused that mark?" I asked curiously.

Grandpa looked up at Kyle and me and turned to Dad.

"That mark is the most special to me. It's the mark your dad helped put on."

As Grandpa talked, that old gun started to come to life. No longer was it a rusted old single-shot. It was a piece of history, my family history.

"That mark your Uncle Tom and I added together," Dad said with a smile. "We had gone hunting the weekend before the state championship game. We shot a couple squirrels and rabbits that weekend. It was an amazing time."

"Dad, that was a long time ago. How come there haven't been any marks added to it since? I'm sure you shot things with it since then," Kyle asked.

Dad put his head down and then looked out toward Grandpa's pasture.

"No, actually that's the last time I ever used that gun. Uncle Tom and I haven't hunted together since. That was our last hunt together when we were in high school," Dad said.

Dad added, "Your grandpa gave me this gun as a wedding present when I married his one and only daughter, hoping more notches would be added someday."

I knew that Dad and Uncle Tom used to be

best friends and hunting partners. I couldn't understand why two friends could ever be that close but now so far apart.

Then it hit me. That gun was more than a gun. It was a symbol of our family and our past. Dad had wanted Kyle and me to put our own notches on the gun. Together. Much like he and Uncle Tom had done so many years ago, much like Grandpa and his family had done.

I walked over and grabbed the pieces of the gun. I looked at Kyle. I apologized to my dad and grandpa.

"Kyle, I think it's time for one more notch on this gun!" I said.

~ 15 ~

No one talked on the way home. There was nothing else to be said. Dad could tell that both of us, especially me, finally understood the significance of the old gun. Suddenly, I didn't worry about getting a new fancy gun. This spring I was on another mission.

That night I had a crazy dream. I dreamed that Kyle and I went back in time. I'm not sure what the year was, but I know it was in the 1800s. The best part was we were walking through some type of hunting encampment. The dream seemed so real.

There were all kinds of hunters sitting around campfires, laughing and eating. There were big bucks along with turkeys and other furs hanging from the tents.

Kyle and I had fun looking at it all and talking

to the different hunters. Some had funny accents and barely spoke any English.

As we neared the edge of the camp, there was a strange-looking man on the outside looking in at the camp. He seemed lonely because there were no other campers around him. He sat motionless at his fire with his head down. There were no stories or laughter, just him sitting alone beside a small fire.

I felt bad for this guy. He was missing the fun, the stories, and all the great things that were going on in the camp. I motioned to Kyle to go toward him. There was just something about him, something mysterious that drew me toward him. I could almost feel him calling me toward his tent.

Kyle grabbed my arm and looked at me. I could tell he was nervous, unsure if we should wander away from the safety of the camp.

The guy looked strange, out of place. Nevertheless, I kept walking. The closer I got to his tent, the faster my heart was beating.

When I reached the man, he slowly looked up. IT WAS UNCLE TOM!

I jumped back, slipping in the wet spring leaves. He stood up and pointed. At first, I thought he was pointing at Kyle. But he wasn't. He was pointing away from the camp, toward an open field to the east. I looked and saw nothing. I looked again and finally saw it.

A giant turkey was strutting around with a flock of hens. The turkey looked brilliant in the field, like a king watching over his castle. The bird stopped and turned, looking in our direction. When he did, I noticed something was odd about his head. There was a big scar running down his face!

The turkey glared. He had a mean look in his eye, as if we were invading his world. Then he gobbled. I don't mean a regular gobble. He gobbled, and it shook the entire woods.

It shook my world! Rain started to pour down and lightning flashed in the distance. I had never seen clouds so fierce yet so amazing.

One more gobble, and I woke up. I jumped from my bed, soaked in sweat. I was drenched, like I had been out in a rainstorm. I looked at the clock and saw it was 5:24 a.m. I couldn't keep this dream to myself and went over to Kyle's bed.

"Are you awake?" I asked as I nudged his arm. He moaned and turned over. I pushed a little harder and actually pushed him out of his bed.

"What in the world?" Kyle asked as he stumbled into our dresser.

"I had a dream," I said excitedly.

"That's great, but why did you wake me up, Kent?" he asked.

"I think I know where the fur-trading encampment is on our property. I know where we need to look!"

Now I had his interest.

"Where?" Kyle shot back.

"Grab a light, and I'll show you. That's not all. I know that huge turkey is still around somewhere. I have to get Scarface with that old .16-gauge. I think it's part of my destiny!" I said.

If we were going to be the ones who found the treasure, we needed to be on the lookout for Uncle Tom and T.J. who were desperately trying to beat us to the punch.

~ 16 ~

The sun hadn't broken over the horizon yet. We snuck through the hallway and out the back door that faced our woods.

"Let's leave our flashlights off until we clear the back barn, just in case Dad heard us leaving," I said.

Kyle agreed, and we made our way through the yard toward the small woodlot by the river. We had just cleared the barn when we heard strange noises.

We both froze and then ducked behind a bush. I couldn't quite make out the voices, but there were definitely two people talking toward the back of our property. I squinted in the darkness and could make out a faint flashlight beam near the creek. My initial instincts told me to go back to the house, that we would be safe there.

I thought about waking Dad and catching whoever was trespassing on our land. However, if I did that, Dad would know that we had snuck out and that we were searching for something.

The wet spring air hung over our heads like an uncomfortable hat. We were a couple days into turkey season, and the weather was warming up.

The damp smell started to overshadow the noises, so Kyle shook me, bringing me back on task. I whispered a plan in Kyle's ear, and we both started to sneak toward the noise, using the river as our guide. As we got closer, I saw two people, one much taller than the other. They were looking at something, but I couldn't tell what it was. We crawled a little closer. I had to hear what they were saying.

"Hold the map still," a voice whispered.

"I am, Dad! This map doesn't make any sense. This is stupid. Can we just go home?"

"Shut up and quit whining. Aren't you sick of playing a secondary role to those boys? This is something that belongs to us, to our family," the voice responded.

"But aren't they our family too, Dad?" the other voice asked.

"Not to me they aren't!" the voice quickly chimed back.

Map? Dad?

"Unreal!" Kyle whispered."It's Uncle Tom and T.J.!"

My blood started to boil. I knew exactly what was happening. T.J. and his dad had the piece of the map from school, and they were trying to find our treasure! Nothing was going to stop them, not even trespassing or stealing. That is so typical of Uncle Tom.

"Hurry up; the sun will be coming up soon," Uncle Tom said.

"I'm trying; this is where the map shows it. I think we really need the other piece," T.J. said.

They both stopped.

"How are we going to do that? They aren't just going to give it to us," Uncle Tom said.

"Then we just take it. No one tells us no," T.J. declared.

With that, they rolled the map up and started

walking toward the other end of our property. They were just about out of sight when they stopped and turned toward us.

Their flashlights started coming right at us. We ducked down behind the bush even more. The lights got closer and closer. Then the pair stopped. For a second, I thought they'd seen us. I thought about running but didn't see the sense in that. I was thinking about just standing up and yelling at them about trespassing on our property.

"Where is it? How could you drop it?" Uncle Tom asked.

They started pawing around the ground, looking for something. They were working their way closer and closer to where we were.

I could almost reach out and grab them. They were coming right toward us. It would be only a matter of seconds before they ran into us.

Suddenly, there was a loud rustling noise to our left. Uncle Tom and T.J. stopped and turned their lights toward the sound. A pair of eyes glowed as the light shown brightly in that direction.

Kyle and I were wondering what kind of animal it was. A raccoon? A coyotc? The animal started walking closer and closer, and then finally revealed itself.

A skunk! It was heading straight at us.

~ 17 ~

Uncle Tom and T.J. started to back away, but it was too late. It was too late for all of us because the skunk squirted so fast. He got Kyle and me behind the bush as well as T.J. and Uncle Tom. What a horrible smell! We did a good job of staying quiet, even with the nauseous odor.

T.J. howled at the smell and Uncle Tom groaned. They began running as fast as they could. I never thought Uncle Tom could move so quickly.

In a way, the skunk saved us, but we paid a terrible price. The odor was everywhere, and the chubby skunk turned and proudly waddled his way toward the woods. He seemed pleased he was ridding the forest of some trespassers.

"The smell! What are we going to do?" Kyle gasped.

I knew what I was going to do. I needed to find out what Uncle Tom and T.J. were looking for. What made them turn around and come back? It must have been something important, something they didn't want to leave behind.

"It's going to be light in a couple of minutes. Let's stay and try and figure out what they were looking for," I said.

About ten minutes later, the sun peeked over the horizon and brought the woods back to life. Kyle looked at his watch and cocked his head. I knew what he was thinking. We were going to be late for school, and we both stank. We sat down against a nearby tree. I looked at Kyle and started to laugh. He started laughing too. We both smelled horrible but what an adventure!

Kyle and I started looking in the leaves where Uncle Tom and T.J. had been looking. Since it was light now, it only took us a couple minutes to find what they had been so anxiously looking for.

Kyle grabbed it and held it up. We both laughed. I was so glad we had stayed to find the missing object. Now I knew why they were so worried. I couldn't believe it. It was Uncle Tom's cell phone and that cell phone was something he couldn't live without. Plus it was evidence that they had been trespassing on our land, trying to take something from us.

"This is better than gold!" I told Kyle.

"I think I know a way we can get the other part of the map, the side we need to find the encampment," I said with a mischievous grin.

~ 18 ~

We rushed into the house as fast as we could and started to get cleaned up for school. But no matter how much soap we used, we couldn't get rid of the stench.

When we sat down at the kitchen table, Mom looked at us strangely and asked, "What on earth is that smell? Did you boys hug a skunk?"

I looked at Kyle, and he looked at me.

"Yeah, we were outside this morning and got sprayed."

Mom filled our plates with pancakes and sausages and went back to the stove to finish hers. Kyle and I started talking about school to keep her from asking questions as we quickly polished off the pancakes. We got up as soon as we were done just as she was about to join us.

"Sorry, we'd love to tell you more, Mom, but

we have to catch the bus," Kyle said. With that, we both grabbed one last pancake and headed out the door. Whew!

As we crossed the front porch, I heard a loud noise. I thought it was the brakes on the bus, so we ran faster toward the bus stop. I noticed that the sky was starting to darken. It was almost as if we were going back in time, back to the darkness of the morning.

Then I saw lightning. BOOM! Thunder exploded from behind us. Another spring Nebraska storm was approaching Bellsville. I felt hopeful that the rain might help get rid of some of the skunk smell that still lingered on us.

We left the house so quickly that we made it to the bus stop a couple minutes early. While we were waiting, we heard another loud noise, but this time we knew it wasn't the bus.

I thought it was thunder, but it wasn't. I looked at Kyle and his eyes were as big as plates. I heard the sound again.

GOBBLE! GOBBLE! It was HIM; it was Scarface appearing right before a storm again!

Where did this turkey live? Where did he hide? The questions kept haunting me. I couldn't figure it out. Wherever it was, it was a great spot. And why did he show up only before storms?

The thunder boomed in the background, and Scarface would respond with a thunder gobble of his own. Turkeys are known as thunder chickens. Now I knew why. It wasn't unusual for a turkey to thunder gobble during a thunderstorm.

The bus arrived, and we got on. Everyone stared at us and held their noses as we walked by. The whispers started, but we didn't care. Kyle and I just wanted to get to school and put our plan in motion. The bus pulled up to T.J.'s house, but he wasn't in front.

The bus slowly pulled away. We needed T.J. for our plan to work so we hoped he'd come to school today despite what happened this morning. The bus came to its usual screeching halt as we pulled up to school. Kyle and I went through the main entrance and headed toward our lockers.

We had math first hour. We were playing a

partner game called Fraction Attack, and Kyle was my partner.

We took a seat in the back corner of the room because we still stank. Even though we had sprayed on a pound of cover-up cologne, the smell still lingered. Just before class began, the door opened and in walked T.J. He wouldn't make eye contact with us but walked by and took his seat on the other side of the room.

We were given an assignment and started working quickly. I could hear T.J. sniffing around. I turned and saw him smelling himself. He thought the smell was coming from him! It was, but little did he know he wasn't the only one who had been sprayed that morning.

T.J. got up, whispered something to the teacher, and left. I looked at Kyle with a grin. Two minutes later, the bell rang. The rest of the morning moved slowly, but we finally made it to lunch.

T.J. returned just in time to go to the cafeteria. It was time to put our plan in motion. Kyle and I ducked into the library and went toward the kids' book section in the back. It was full of kids' books and a small puppet theater, a great place to hide. I had used the space often when I was trying to avoid homework assignments or the principal.

Once we got back there, I pulled the cell phone out of my book bag. It was an expensive, fancy one, the only phone that was worthy enough for the great Tom Titus.

I started to scroll through his contacts until I came to the one I had been looking for and hit the call button.

"Hey, Dad. You found your phone!" a voice whispered on the other end.

"No, T.J.! This isn't your Daddy. It's Kent. I have his phone, and we saw you early this morning. We know what you were doing," I said.

Sudden silence.

"What do you want, Kent?" T.J. demanded.

Finally, I had something T.J. wanted, something he couldn't buy.

"So glad you asked. Two things actually. The first is for you and your dad to keep away our property," I said. Before T.J. could answer, I added, "The second thing I want is the other half of the map."

I could tell this was something T.J. had to think about. He wasn't used to not being able to get everything he wanted. I don't think his dad had ever said no to him.

After a minute, I asked, "Do we have a deal or not? I can easily take this phone to the police and tell them where I found it. I can go into detail about how we saw people trespassing on our land early this morning and we found one of their cell phones. You make the call," I said.

"Fine, deal. Meet me at the water vending machine in five minutes," T.J. said.

I hung up and winked at Kyle. We walked out and put our textbooks in our lockers and then headed toward the water machine.

T.J. was there waiting for us. As we walked up, he started sniffing again. Now he knew we had really seen them, not just by having the cell phone but also by the familiar skunk smell.

"Here," T.J. said as he handed us the old map.

We thanked him, and I gave him his dad's cell phone. He grabbed it and hurried off down the hall.

Kyle and I quickly opened the map. I couldn't believe what I was looking at. The map showed us something that I never would have thought of, something that was going to help us unlock the unusual mystery and point us in the right direction to find our treasure. This whole time we had been hoping to find artifacts from the old fur trading post, but there was more, much more.

There was a hidden treasure on our farm, a treasure that was worth more than money, a treasure that would forever change all of our lives.

Right there on the map was what I had hoped for all along. Finding the other half of the map confirmed what I thought I had seen in Mr. Potter's classroom.

There *was* a big red X. The treasure was going to be ours!

~ 19 ~

The last hour's bell couldn't ring fast enough. Friday always seemed to be the slowest day of the school week. I watched as the clock slowly crept closer to our three o'clock dismissal. I was so glad it was Friday. Kyle and I would need the weekend to find the treasure. I was convinced we would have it before school resumed on Monday.

The bell finally rang, and we raced toward the bus. We immediately sat down, waiting for the bus to pull away. Kids started to climb aboard, but there was no sign of T.J.

"Look who's suddenly missing," Kyle said sarcastically.

I scanned the schoolyard, playground, and front steps, looking for any sign of T.J. The principal gave the all-clear message over the radio and our bus just started to pull out without him when we heard a strange message come on the radio.

"Bus 7: Mr. Tron, please pull off for a safety check."

Safety check? Now? We had to get home and find the treasure. We usually have one safety check per year, and we already had this year's.

As we pulled off into the bus garage, I felt Kyle's bony elbow in my side.

"Look!" he said, pointing out his window toward the school.

There was T.J. climbing into his father's convertible. We watched them speed off quickly. Wherever they were going, they were in a major hurry.

"Boy, that's odd," I said to Kyle.

"Not odd, more like planned," Kyle whispered.

After we spent awhile in the garage, the bus finally took off again. We were on our way home, but for some reason today, we were going to get there a little later than usual.

The ride seemed like it was taking forever because we were so anxious to start our treasure hunt. After the bus finally dropped us off, we ran in the door and headed to our rooms. I looked at the clock. It said four-thirty, and we usually got home around three-fifty. Today we really were late.

It had to have been the work of Uncle Tom and T.J. We were sure that they somehow had the bus delayed at the school. Besides that, Mr. Tron's route had taken extra long today.

Oh well, we didn't have time to worry about that. What was done was done. The important thing was that we finally had the entire map in our possession.

Kyle took his hand and brushed off everything on top of our desk and clicked on his Nebraska Cornhusker desk lamp. I reached in my pocket and pulled out the piece of the map we had found this morning. It was old and brittle; there was no doubt about it. A corner piece broke off as I unfolded it. Luckily, the piece had no writing on it, so I quickly set it aside.

I combined it with the section we had gotten from T.J. at lunch. Since the map was in French and neither of us had taken the language, we started examining it for any clues to help us find the treasure.

We'd learned in our history class that many early explorers were from France and had come to get rich off the New World's vast treasure of furs. So we were sure something valuable was connected with the map.

"We were looking in the wrong spot, and so were T.J. and Uncle Tom!" Kyle finally said. I looked at him and back at the map. Kyle took his finger and pointed at the first bend in the river where we'd looked.

We thought we'd been looking in the right spot. He traced the twisting, turning path of the river on the map. Then he looked at me and smirked. I knew what that smile meant. Now we both knew where we had to look, and it wasn't even close to the spot where we'd been that morning.

You needed both pieces of the map to see it. The spot wasn't hidden. It was in our own back-yard!

~ 20 ~

That night we celebrated our birthday. Even though our actual birthday wasn't until Wednesday, our parents decided to celebrate it early. After dinner, we all went into the living room, and Mom gave us an oblong box wrapped in red and gray paper with a nice silver bow on top. I could tell that Mom had really taken her time to wrap it extra special.

It had to be either a gun or a metal detector. I had bugged Mom and Dad so much about getting a new gun I thought that was probably what it was.

"Go ahead, boys. Open it up. Happy birthday!" Dad said. I looked at him, and he was smiling. I knew either way, he was proud of whatever it was.

After talking with Grandpa, I had already

made up my mind that no matter what, Kyle and I were going to put the thirteenth slash on the stock of the gun when I killed Scarface.

Mom placed the box on our laps, and we tore into it. Much to my surprise, it was a brand new metal detector! It was awesome, better than anything I could have imagined.

"I took the shotgun back yesterday. I think this is a great gift and figured you wanted to try that old, single-shot a few more times," Dad said with a smile.

He knew we had finally understood about the old gun and how important it was to add the slash. We didn't need a new gun just yet.

With the metal detector, we finally had everything we'd need to become real treasure hunters. And we knew the first place we'd look.

On really wet, spring days, the river would flood and provide Kyle and me with some excitement when we were younger. The overflow water would form a creek and flow across our backyard and reconnect with the river again farther downstream. Sometimes the water would get so deep we could jump into it off our back porch.

Dad told us how when we were younger, there used to be a good fishing hole near where our house was built. He also told us how that all had changed about five years earlier when the city put a small dam near that part of the river. After that, we never had water in our backyard, and it actually changed the river's natural flow.

The water was diverted toward town to help provide water for the treatment plant. However, on rainy spring days, we would still get a little water in the backyard, reminding my dad of those early days.

That spot is right where the encampment was! We had finally figured it out. Our house was actually built right near the early fur trading post where the river used to flow!

The next morning finally came, and we were up early. We sprinted toward the garage, grabbed our new metal detector and walked out the back door headed for the river. We turned the detector on and started scanning as we neared the water.

We walked another couple hundred yards and didn't have any hits on the machine. I looked at Kyle dumbfounded. If the encampment was here, there would have been a ton of old artifacts that would make the detector go crazy. Unfortunately we made it to the river without a single buzz or beep.

We spent hours combing the edges of the river. We worked the area where we thought the bend would be and the river had been dammed. You could tell because erosion had taken its toll and there were much smaller, younger trees, a vast difference from the oaks and hardwoods littering both sides of the river.

Something wasn't right. We pulled out the map again.

"This is the second bend," Kyle said.

"I know, I know. It doesn't make any sense." I started to twist and turn the map.

"Stop! Turn it back the way you just had it," Kyle said.

I slowly turned the map vertically and quickly found our mistake. The whole time we'd been looking at the map like a textbook. Since we couldn't make out any of the writing, we weren't sure which way to hold it. Now it was clear—we needed to move downstream. We had to follow the river past our house toward the road.

We started jogging down the river with the metal detector strapped over my shoulder.

BEEP! I stopped and froze.

It was our metal detector, which I had forgotten was even on.

BEEP! BEEP!

~ 21 ~

Kyle quickly bent down and started to dig with his hands.

"This is going to take forever. Go back to the garage and grab a shovel," I told Kyle.

He was off. Boy, was he a fast runner. I chuckled to myself as I watched him. The sun cast a unique glow over his red hair as he smoothly sprinted back to the house.

I continued to dig by hand. I had gotten down about six inches when my hand hit something hard. I stopped and slowly started to brush the coarse black dirt off whatever it was. I couldn't tell, but there was definitely something there.

The more I brushed, the more letters I could see. I slowly pulled it out. Soda can.

It was an old can but not quite what we were looking for. I sat down and laughed at myself. I really thought we'd found something from the encampment. We were digging for hope, for a sign.

After a couple minutes, Kyle returned panting.

"I got the shovel. Do you find what set off the detector?"

I held up my proud find—an old battered can.

He let out a long sigh and sat down on the stump next to me. It was lunch time now and boy were we hungry. After lunch we had promised to do some chores for Dad. We really didn't have any more time to search.

We had planned to go turkey hunting again the next morning before church. I had almost forgotten with all the excitement of our treasure hunt.

"Do you think we'll see Scarface again?" Kyle asked.

I nodded. I had no doubt that somehow, somewhere, we were going to run into Scarface.

"Let's go home. We can look again tomorrow after we get in from hunting," I told Kyle.

We walked up the riverbank toward the house.

Suddenly my right toe caught on something and I went tumbling. Luckily, Kyle was carrying the metal detector or it would have broken. I could hear him laughing as I pulled myself up and brushed off my clothes.

"Stupid root," I muttered as I reached back to kick it.

When my foot hit it, it moved. I stopped and looked at Kyle who was a couple steps behind me.

When I pulled on it, the object shifted. It was buried deep, so I called Kyle over with the shovel. By the time he finished digging around it and had the clump of dirt removed, Mom was calling us in for lunch. Whatever it was, it was about four to five inches long. We were very close to our house, about a hundred yards away in a small thicket of young trees. I continued to get several strong hits on the detector as we neared our backyard.

When we got to the water spigot on the side of the house, we washed off the clay soil clinging to it and saw the object we dug out was a fork. Not just a fork, but a really, old one.

It wasn't the treasure we had been looking for, but it was solid evidence that there was something unique and historical about our property.

We were about to find out there was more to this treasure hunt than we ever imagined.

~ 22 ~

Morning couldn't come soon enough. That night I had trouble sleeping again. I had weird dreams about the French encampment, and I couldn't stop thinking about Scarface. Ever since our encounter, I had my mind set on that turkey. He was like nothing I had ever seen before. Not only was his beard massive, so was he.

Our love for turkey hunting started when we were young. Dad took us into the spring woods where he taught us about the different types of turkey calls. There was nothing we loved more than when we would hear a tom gobble.

Hunting turkeys hooked us at a very young age. It stirred us then, and it still makes my heart race even though we now are in high school.

The night before there were so many things on my mind that it was hard to fall asleep, but I finally did. The last time I had looked at my alarm clock it was 2 a.m.

Even so, I was up before my alarm. I glanced out my window and saw that was still dark, but I could smell fresh bacon and eggs when I stumbled into the kitchen.

"Good morning, Son," Dad said with a smile.

"Morning," I grunted as I went to the fridge. Kyle was already up and eating. He was a morning person and always seemed so awake then, not like me.

He loved bacon. Once he smelled it, he jumped out of bed and ran to the kitchen. I was the opposite. I could stay up all night, but there were few things I hated more than mornings. For some strange reason, though, I could get up pretty easily if it had anything to do with hunting.

Dad was making his special chocolate chip pancakes, a family favorite. We sat down and after Dad said a prayer, we laughed and talked about where we would be hunting.

I really loved this time with my dad and brother. Hunting is so much fun, but I really enjoyed the time leading up to the hunt. The plan was set. Kyle and I were going to hunt the northwest side of the property, near the creek. Dad was going to hunt on the east side. Since the old .16 gauge was broken, we had to take Kyle's old gun.

"Boys, keep your eyes peeled for old Scarface. I've got a feeling he's still around," Dad said.

"How do you know that, Dad? He could have already got shot or moved on to another property," I said.

Kyle added, "Dad, there hasn't been any sign of him in awhile."

Dad chuckled and looked toward the horizon.

"I've been doing this a lot longer than both of you. I don't have any evidence, just a feeling," Dad said.

I really loved turkey hunting, although I do also like to deer hunt. My ultimate passion is being in the woods in the spring.

It was nice not to have to worry about our scent. During deer season, we don't have a big breakfast because of a deer's sense of smell.

Turkeys are not blessed with a deer's nose, but they do have amazing eyesight. I've been busted many times trying to sneak up and shoot a turkey. It's very difficult. Today we went out to the garage smelling of crispy bacon and pancakes in the damp spring air.

Our flashlights helped Kyle and I make our way toward our blind, and we watched as Dad set out with a lantern for his. We all settled in with lots of time before sunrise.

As we listened to the wonderful sounds of spring, we heard our first gobble just after sunrise. It wasn't too close, coming between where we were and where Dad's blind was.

Before long, the air filled with many gobbles. It was beautiful to our hunters' ears, better than any music I'd ever heard. But even with all of them, one was missing. No Scarface, I was sure of that. There was no mistaking his gobble. Kyle and I talked beforehand, and he knew I was going to wait for Scarface. I told him that Scarface was the only turkey I'd put my tag on.

About an hour after sunrise, we heard some

turkeys working their way through the woods toward us. We had set out two decoys—a jake and hen—in front of us. The hens saw them and didn't seem to mind. I let out a couple of yelps and a gobbler instantly called back.

I did a couple more calls, and suddenly saw a bright red head appear over a small hill. The tom instantly started strutting when he saw our decoys. I made a couple yelps on my mouth call followed by a very hard, aggressive cut. That got his attention.

He turned and headed right toward the decoys. I glanced at Kyle, and he was set. The gun was up, and he was ready. Once the bird passed the first window of our blind, he started to strut again. There is hardly a better sight than a strutting tom in the spring. They look so majestic and so powerful.

The bird put on a beautiful display of dominance and danced. He stopped and then went toward the jake decoy. I could see him turn one more time. Then I heard the roar of the old .16 gauge. The bird flipped over twice, kicked, and was done!

Kyle and I began whooping and hollering. We hugged and he ran out to grab his bird. It was a great turkey with a ten-inch beard and big spurs more than an inch long. I could tell he was an old one.

Kyle threw the bird over his shoulder, and we went back toward the house. I could see Dad's smile as we neared the back door. He had heard the shot and come to join us at the house.

"Great job, Kyle!" Dad said, giving us both a high five.

"What about you, Son? Don't you want to get back out there? We have a lot more turkeys on the property," said Dad.

"We have something to—" I said but stopped myself. I quickly added, "Dad, there's only one turkey on my mind this spring."

It was the truth. But there was something else lurking in the back of my mind.

Before I could say a word, Kyle had gone to the garage and was already looking for another shovel. We now had two shovels and daylight.

Dad jumped in the truck to run breakfast over to Grandpa and Grandma's house. He was just about out of the driveway when his truck suddenly stopped. Kyle and I looked toward the road as a fancy, red convertible sports car zoomed past.

It was Uncle Tom, and he wasn't alone.

~ 23 ~

T.J! I could tell by the look on Dad's face he wasn't happy that they were nosing around. Granted, there were a couple other houses on our road but not many. We all knew that they were up to something. Dad just scratched his head and turned down the road toward Grandpa's.

Kyle and I knew what they were doing. Or maybe I should say knew what they were looking for. There was no time to waste.

We knew they would be sneaking around looking for the treasure. It was just like them. They were already the richest family in town, but it wasn't good enough. Nothing was ever good enough for my uncle.

Sometimes in the past I had felt bad for T.J. but not anymore. T.J. was turning into his father the older we got. When we were younger, we used to be friends. It was always awkward, but at least his parents used to let us play together in school and when we visited our grandparents.

But not lately. Ever since we started junior high, things had become even worse between T.J. and us. Sports were a big part of it. Both Kyle and I were athletic; sports came easy to us.

Even though they didn't come easy for T.J., his dad always thought he should be the star of the team. One time Uncle Tom paid a full-time trainer to try to make T.J. into a super athlete. Unfortunately for him, it didn't work.

Uncle Tom would come to games and scream and yell, although I have to admit T.J. did seem embarrassed. But T.J. was spoiled and acted like a baby whenever he didn't get his way. After he stole our map, I had pretty much written him off as a cousin.

This treasure hunting adventure was one thing his dad couldn't buy or take from us. It was our treasure to find.

"I wonder if there are gold coins," I said.

"Gold, silver, could be anything. I know one

thing—just thinking of the word treasure gets me excited," Kyle said.

The map couldn't lie. There was a huge X on it, so it had to be some kind of special treasure. We both laughed and dreamed as we walked toward the spot where we'd found the fork.

As we got closer, I flipped on the metal detector and started getting hits instantly; the beeping was out of control.

Kyle took the shovel and started digging. After a couple inches, there was a loud clunk. Kyle quickly dug around the object and pulled it out. No treasure, but it was something old. We wiped the dirt off and discovered an old pot, probably used by guys before a morning hunt.

The history of Bellsville was coming alive to us, and Kyle and I had a front row seat. The pot wasn't what we were expecting, but it was still cool. We continued to dig around.

We found many relics, from buttons to buckles. After hours of searching, we had about ten items in a small bucket. No treasure, though, or at least that's what we thought.

~ 24 ~

We had definitely found evidence of an early encampment, so the map was real. There had to be something valuable where the red X was located. I had no doubt there was a treasure hidden in Bellsville, and it was on our property.

We took the items we found down to the stream to wash them off. There was silverware, pieces of metal, and an old key.

The key was somewhat cool. The shape was unique, but you could tell it had been used as a key at one time. It reminded me of a turkey foot. Maybe I just had Scarface on my mind.

"That's cool," Kyle said.

"Yeah, I guess, it would be even cooler if it opened the vault to the bank downtown," I laughed.

Kyle laughed too. If nothing else, we were

explorers. What we found so far were historical items that helped shape our city. We headed back to the house to get ready for church. We laughed and joked about our treasure hunting skills.

We were flipping the key back and forth, playing catch with it. Kyle took it and threw it behind his back toward me. I fumbled it and dropped it. Kyle knelt down to pick it up.

I stood there laughing when Kyle pointed. He had a smart smirk on his face, the kind that meant he was on to something big.

"Look," he slowly mumbled.

I went down to my knees and looked in the direction that he was pointing. At first, I didn't see it. "What?"

"Just look over there!"

I stared. There were a number of trees that separated our house and the field where we were. I scanned the area looking for something that would catch my attention. Then I saw it. Just as clear as a blue Nebraska summer day, I saw it— the tree, the same one that had been hit by lightning and that we once thought was burnt and worthless, had taken on a new shape. I tilted my head and looked at it the way Kyle was looking. From the ground where we were, it looked much differently. All those days of glancing out our window, I always looked past the tree.

Now from a new perspective, the trunk and branches looked like a hand pointing down. There was no doubt about it.

We both were spellbound, in awe of how the tree was giving us a sign, and walked over to it. I looked at Kyle and smiled; he still had that smirk.

"Hand me the metal detector," I told him.

He reached and pulled the detector off his back. Just as I went to flip it on, there was a loud beeping noise. At first, I thought it was the detector, but it wasn't. The noise was coming from behind us, down by the river.

We started jogging toward it. It got louder and louder. When we reached the river, we caught movement across to the east. It looked like trees were falling down. Animals were running in all directions. The noise was loud and heading toward us.

- 25 -

A bulldozer. And a backhoe. They were both ripping and tearing their way toward our location at the creek. We knew instantly who was behind it. The logo on the side of both machines quickly confirmed what we already knew. It was Titus Construction Company.

They were clearing the land across the river. Once they reached the river, they put the machines in neutral and waited while the machines idled at an evil roar. Within minutes, Uncle Tom and T.J. came cruising down on a couple four-wheelers. They pulled in, parked their ATVs, and started talking to the people driving the big machines.

We just stood there. Uncle Tom looked at us once, smirked, and looked away. T.J. turned to look at us and laughed.

My blood started to boil, and I could feel my face start to turn bright red.

"Calm down, don't let them get to you," Kyle said quietly.

How could I calm down! I knew why they were there. They were looking for the treasure, our treasure. It seemed like they always had to have everything. I was sick of it. I couldn't take it anymore.

I reached down and picked up a rock. I wound up as I never had before and let my arm go. Just before the rock left my hand, I felt Kyle's hand grab mine. The rock fell safely into the river with a big splash, which caused everyone on the other side to stop.

"You boys got a problem?" Uncle Tom yelled.

We didn't say a word. There were so many things I wanted to yell at them, but somehow, I stopped myself.

"Why don't you boys bring those shovels over here? I'll pay you to help us dig," Uncle Tom said. "I could probably pay you more than your old man makes at his hardware store job!"

I couldn't take it anymore.

"I hate you! And you too, T.J." I yelled.

As soon as I said it, I regretted it. Not so much for my Uncle Tom but for T.J. Even as awful as he was, I knew I shouldn't have said it. I could tell when I said those hateful words, it bothered him.

"Let's get out of here, Kent," Kyle said, grabbing my arm. I looked back one more time as we cleared the riverbank. The last thing I saw was Uncle Tom pointing at T.J., and he didn't look very happy. We ran to our house and called Dad.

"Sorry, boys, but there's nothing I can do. Uncle Tom probably has permission to be on our neighbor's land. He isn't trespassing our land. I'm really sorry, boys," Dad said.

I couldn't believe it. There was a part of me that wanted my dad to come down, wade across the river, and grab Uncle Tom by the neck to teach him a lesson and beat him up. I thought that would make me feel better.

"Dad, that's it? That's all you're going to do? I can't believe that! He disrespected you," I said angrily.

There was a long pause on the phone. For a second, I thought my dad had hung up on me for raising my voice. I was trying my best not to be emotional, not to cry. My heart seemed like it was beating harder and louder than any bulldozer.

"Kent, I actually feel bad for him, for both of them," Dad finally said.

What? Feel bad? Feel bad for the richest, most arrogant man in the world, the man who just trashed our family, someone who has done nothing but hurt my dad for years?

"I just keep praying and hoping he changes someday," Dad said.

After we hung up, a part of me was still wondering why Dad hadn't done anything. He should have handled it like a man. I sat picking at my fingers. I started to bite my fingernails and spit out pieces of skin. I always did that when I was nervous before a big game or when I thought I was in trouble.

"Maybe Dad's right," Kyle said.

"Right about what?" I asked.

I started to calm down and think about it. Kyle

just shook his head. We sat on the back porch and watched as the heavy equipment knocked down trees and dug into the ground across the river.

"You know, they're looking on the wrong side of the river," Kyle said.

Finally I could laugh. I had forgotten. T.J. had been looking at the map upside down just as we had done in the beginning. They thought the encampment and treasure were on the north side of our property. They weren't. They were digging for nothing. I couldn't help but smile.

Occasionally T.J. would look over toward us as the big machines continued digging. You could see Uncle Tom getting more upset by the minute as they rummaged through the dirt.

Nothing. They found nothing, and they weren't going to because they were digging in the wrong spot!

"Let's go back to the tree and turn on the metal detector. I know there's something hidden under that tree," I said to Kyle.

Kyle looked at me and looked at all the noisy equipment.

"Not now, just in case they see us. We're going to have to come back after dark," Kyle said.

Good idea, I thought.

"I guess we won't be hunting down there tomorrow anyway. With all the noise they're making, Scarface is probably in a different state," I said.

~ 26 ~

Kyle and I kept peeking out our bedroom window, waiting for the red lights on top of the bulldozer to stop the blinking. It was about eleven-thirty when they finally stopped.

We had left all our digging equipment on the back porch so we wouldn't make any noise. We opened our bedroom window and crawled out. The spring night was beautiful. There were a million stars shining, reminding me of fireflies near the river in the summer.

I stood for a second admiring the sights and smells of spring, then took a deep breath and grabbed the metal detector. Kyle picked up his shovel, and we headed toward the twisted burnt tree.

I took a deep breath and turned on the metal detector. As I continued around the tree, the beeping got more frequent and louder. When I reached the side of the tree that faced the river, the detector began going crazy.

I quickly shut it off. I nodded to Kyle, and he pushed his shovel in and scooped out some dirt. After a couple more shovels of dirt, the color of the dirt started to change so we knew we probably were close. We knew how deep we had dug to find the other artifacts down by the river and figured the treasure would be buried the same distance down.

"Here, you finish," Kyle said, trying to hand me the shovel.

That was Kyle, always worrying about me. He has a gift of making everyone else feel special.

"No, Kyle, you go ahead and finish."

"No, I insist. Now grab the shovel and let's find our treasure," Kyle said.

With that, I took the old wooden-handled shovel from him. It's hard to describe the feeling when I grasped that shovel. In my heart, I knew we were inches away from our treasure. I felt powerful as I slammed the shovel in the dirt.

The first scoop was nothing but dirt. When I put the shovel in the dirt for a second time, there was a loud thud. I hit something. I reached down and pulled on the object. At first, it wouldn't budge, but I rocked it back and forth in the hole until it started to break free from the dirt and gently pulled it up. We both just stood there staring.

It was some type of chest but not just an ordinary one; it was obviously old. The box was about the size of my lunch tray at school. It was about five inches deep and had a lock on it.

We rushed to the back porch to see it under the light. I took off my shirt and wiped the box off. It was made of some type of metal and had carvings of animals on it—a huge buck, a black bear, and a turkey. The box was still sealed tight with a padlock.

I held it up and examined it more carefully. There was something written on the bottom. I wiped off more dirt until I could make it out.

"What do you see? What's it say?" Kyle asked.

I stared at it.

"What's it say?" Kyle asked again.

"It looks like it says 'Pardonner.'"

"Huh?" Kyle answered dumbfounded. "I don't know who this Pardonner is, but I bet he was rich."

~ 27 ~

I was intrigued by the name Pardonner but really wanted to see what was inside the mysterious box. The name didn't sound familiar, but that didn't mean he wasn't famous.

There was something mysterious about the old box. I looked at the lock and examined it. After all these years, the mysterious ancient lock still protected its treasure. The last thing I wanted to do was break something so old.

We could tell that someone took a lot of time making it. Whoever did it wanted to protect what was in it. We quietly snuck back into the house and slid the box under my bed. We figured if we had waited that long, it wouldn't hurt to wait until morning.

"I bet there's a bunch of gold coins," I whispered.

Kyle shrugged and smiled. It didn't matter what was inside. We had found IT! It was ours, and it was something special.

As I drifted off to sleep, I couldn't help but think about T.J. I could tell I had hurt him. At first I thought yelling at him would make me feel better, but it hadn't. I actually felt worse.

Maybe Dad was right about ignoring the whole thing. He would always tell us to make sure we took the high road, but today I hadn't.

It was weird to have two extremely different emotions. On the one hand, I was filled with excitement over the treasure chest, but on the other hand, I felt guilty for the way I reacted to Uncle Tom's taunting. That night I barely slept. I was starting to wonder if all this was worth it.

I kept tossing and turning with more crazy dreams about gold and silver and buying a mansion. In my dream, I bought all Uncle Tom's companies, and I owned all Bellsville, but I still wasn't happy. I wanted more. When I woke up, I was drenched in sweat and glad to hear the neighbor's rooster crowing.

Would money and fame make me like Uncle Tom?

It was just breaking daylight, and everyone was up. Kyle was already getting dressed for school, and I was trying to wake up. I went in to brush my teeth and saw lightning in the distance. I ran to my window and looked toward the back of our property. There were dark clouds bringing another big, Nebraska spring storm.

The first thunder hit close, causing me to almost jump out of my pajamas, it was so loud. Lighting along with loud thunder hit again and again. At first, I didn't think much about it. We get many storms like this during the spring. My mind was on how we were going to get the treasure chest open.

Suddenly I heard another loud boom, but this one was different. It was HIM! It was faint, but I was sure of it. It was Scarface. He was back! I ran to the kitchen where Dad was packing his lunch for work.

"Dad, please let me stay home and go turkey hunting this morning," I begged.

Dad tilted his head sideways and looked at me.

"No way. School is more important. You know that," Dad said. He went back to packing his lunch.

I ran back to my bedroom and looked out the window. Lightning struck and thunder boomed. It was an awesome scene. Then the rain started. It began slowly but quickly turned into a downpour.

Through the rain, I could make out a huge shape moving through the field directly behind our house. I wasn't sure if it was a deer or a turkey.

Then the lightning filled the sky, and this time it lit up the entire field. The animal stopped, looked right at me, and let out a frightening gobble. I knew it was Scarface! I'm not ashamed to admit I was scared. Then he quickly disappeared.

~ 28 ~

"Here comes the bus!" Dad yelled.

I grabbed my coat and headed out the front door. Then I remembered—our secret treasure chest.

"Kyle, the chest! Hold the bus up!" I called, sprinting back to my room.

I grabbed the box and emptied out some of the junk littering my backpack. I shoved the box in and took off out the front door. Luckily Kyle thought of some story to hold the bus up. He smiled his smile, and the bus driver waved as I ran up the steps. I went to my seat.

Kyle leaned over and whispered, "Did you get it?" Kyle asked.

I nodded. We didn't bring it up the rest of the ride to school. We didn't want anyone to hear us talking about our treasure.

The bus pulled in to Bellsville High School, and after getting off, we hurried toward our lockers. I wanted to make sure to keep the chest close by at all times; it was too valuable to part with.

We met at my locker, and I motioned to Kyle to follow me into the restroom. I pulled the chest out of my backpack and put it on the sink. Wow, this thing was cool.

The bathroom lights made the chest glow. Last night in the dark, we hadn't been able to see all the detail. I just knew there was something valuable in it.

I tried to wiggle the lock, but it wouldn't budge. It didn't even move an inch.

"Too bad we don't have the key," I said.

Kyle looked at me and then at the box.

"A key…why didn't I think of it before?" he said. "Kent, we do have a key. It's in the pile of stuff we found in the bucket at home," Kyle said.

The key! We had found a key down by the river. At first, we thought it was just a worthless old key to some dresser or door, but maybe this was the key to unlock the chest. There was one major problem—the key was at home and we were stuck at school. It was only a little after eight o'clock, and we had the whole day to sit and wait.

I didn't think I could wait much longer. Last night had been the longest night of my life. Now today was sure to take forever.

"Since we can't open it, we should at least try to see what the writing means," I said.

Kyle nodded, and we knew there was only one person who could help us figure this out—Mr. Potter.

We didn't have history class until fourth hour, after lunch. Suddenly, I didn't feel comfortable with the chest in my backpack all day. The thought of keeping it with me for four hours seemed like a major problem. I knew my only option was to hide the box somewhere safe.

"We need a safe place to stash this box," I told Kyle.

Kyle started to look around. It seemed like there were no good spots in the entire school. We couldn't risk anyone coming across our treasure. We knew that T.J. would be on the lookout for anything we had, especially today. He'd use all his resources and money to get what was ours.

"What about the garbage?" Kyle said.

The garbage? I couldn't stand the thought of throwing away something we'd worked so hard to find, something so valuable. The more I thought about it, though, it did seem like a good idea.

"Nobody would ever look in the garbage," Kyle said with a smile.

He was right. No one would dig through the garbage, especially in a junior high school. I slipped the chest to Kyle and he walked over to the garbage can near the vending machines. He flipped the lid open, slowly lowered the chest into the can, and let the lid back down.

"There. No one will ever find it now. We'll come back after lunch and take it to Mr. Potter's class," Kyle said.

We both smiled and headed to math class.

Little did we know someone had been watching us the whole time.

~ 29 ~

The morning dragged on and on. It seemed like lunch time would never arrive.

When the third-hour bell finally rang, Kyle and I ran toward our locker. The plan was to stick the chest in my backpack and take it to Mr. Potter's class after lunch. We knew he'd be able to examine the chest and interpret the strange writing. He might even know who this Pardonner was.

Kyle stood watch as I snuck over to the garbage can. I couldn't have anyone see me going through a nasty garbage can. I had a reputation to maintain. I could just imagine the rumors flying around the school about the Morris boys sifting through garbage cans.

We also didn't want to draw any attention to our treasure.

I took some paper out of my binder and walked over to throw it away. I took one more glance over my shoulder, and Kyle gave me the nod. I stuck my hand down to grab the chest.

I started feeling food wrappers, all sorts of debris and other disgusting items, but no chest. It was gone! I started to panic and started rummaging through the entire can. It was disgusting. There was food and trash all over my sleeve.

The chest was gone! I gave Kyle a panicked look. He came over to investigate.

"It's gone!" I whispered to him.

Kyle motioned for me to move out of the way. Since he was much taller and lankier, he had much longer arms. At first, he thought maybe I just missed it and hadn't reached down far enough in the can. He was wrong! He felt around the entire can and could find no chest.

"This isn't good," Kyle said.

Not only was the chest gone, but we were both covered in food and garbage. Kyle had some type of pudding all over his sleeves, and I was coated with an assortment of breakfast leftovers.

"Let's go clean up and make a plan. Someone must have seen us this morning and then taken our treasure!"

The bathroom near our lockers was closed for cleaning, so we went down toward the sophomore hallway. Just as we were about to walk into the bathroom, we heard yelling. We both paused just inside, listening to the commotion, and tried to figure out what was going on.

"You're such a loser! Why don't you cry some more, you little baby?" someone shouted from the last stall.

There was a faint whimpering coming from the stall along with several taunts and jeers.

We got closer and I ducked down to look under the stall. There were three pairs of shoes in one stall, and I could see the top of someone's head. I could tell they were holding someone upside down by his ankles. We'd seen this before. These thugs were going to give this poor kid a swirly.

Whoever it was didn't seem to be enjoying the attention. Most people would walk away from the situation, but we couldn't. One thing that drove both Kyle and me crazy were bullies. We never understood why anyone would want to make someone else feel bad. Our dad had always told us to stick up for other kids. It was never okay to bully anyone or let anyone be bullied.

We quietly stood outside the stall. Then Kyle looked at me and held up three fingers. He counted down, and when he hit zero, we both kicked the stall door in.

The rusty gray door flew open with a loud crash.

We startled the bullies. However, the surprise was actually on us. There was T.J. hanging upside down and cradled in his hand was our chest.

T.J. had stolen our treasure chest.

~ 30 ~

"Oh, hey. It's only Kent and Kyle," one of the boys said.

There were three sophomores, three guys we had played football and basketball with. For a split second, I thought about grabbing our chest and leaving T.J. In my mind, the thief deserved it, but we couldn't.

"Hey, guys. Why don't you leave him alone?"

One of the boys started to say something, but Kyle quickly interrupted him.

"Put him down now, or you're going to have more trouble than you guys want," said Kyle.

When Kyle spoke, people always listened.

"We were just having a little fun with your cousin and his cute little toy box," one bully said.

"Maybe you guys didn't hear us the first time," I replied.

Both Kyle and I had a reputation, and these boys knew it. They didn't want to mess with us.

"Whatever. Let's go, guys. Leave the nerd and his box with his cousins. Maybe they can go out and play together after school," said another boy.

They flipped T.J. around and stood him up. All the boys left the stall and walked out of the bathroom. I could hear the last one say on the way out, "Hello, Mr. Hall." Our principal, Mr. Hall walked in.

"What are you boys doing?" he asked.

We looked around. He had to have heard all the commotion.

"Is there a problem?" Mr. Hall asked T.J.

We all knew that T.J.'s mom was his secretary and that Uncle Tom and Mr. Hall were good friends. This was T.J.'s chance to get us in trouble so he could keep our chest. The dirtball!

The three of us stood there looking at each other. T.J. was surprised we'd come to his rescue. I was burning mad because of the bullies and the fact that T.J. had stolen our treasure chest.

It was an ugly sight.

"We're just working on our history project," T.J. said.

"Yeah. We're just going over some last minute details about a project on early settlers of Bellsville," Kyle added.

"T.J., you sure there isn't a problem?" Mr. Hall asked him again.

Kyle and I looked at T.J. He shook his head. Maybe T.J. wasn't so bad. Maybe somewhere in his skinny, little body he did have a heart.

"Is there any way you could give us a hall pass so we aren't late for class?" Kyle quickly asked.

Mr. Hall laughed, "You're on your own, boys."

I walked over and took the chest out of T.J.'s hand.

- 31 -

The three of us went into Mr. Potter's class late. Everyone was staring at us. We must have been a quite a sight. Kyle and I were still covered in food from digging through the garbage, and T.J. was dripping sweat from the bathroom incident.

Mr. Potter could tell something had been going on, but he just motioned for us to take our seats. He was lecturing on the American Revolution. He spent almost the entire class time explaining the role of women during the Revolution. With about five minutes left in class, he passed out a worksheet.

I sat motionless staring at the clock, watching every second tick closer to the bell. Finally, it rang. The class slowly emptied, but the three of us stayed after.

"Can I help you boys with something?"

The three of us walked up to his desk. I could tell he was trying to make sense of all this. He was very curious why we were with T.J. The whole town knew the Morris family never associated with the Titus family. Ever!

I cautiously unzipped my backpack and pulled out the chest. Mr. Potter's eyes instantly lit up.

"Where did you boys find this? You didn't steal it, did you?" he asked.

"No, it's a long story, but we found it on our property behind our house," I said.

Kyle went on to tell him about his map and the metal detector. T.J. just sat quietly and listened.

Deep down inside he knew he was wrong— wrong for stealing, lying, and plotting against his own family. But T.J. wasn't the only one who was wrong. I was guilty as well. I knew I was wrong for what I had said to him the night before.

It had been eating away at me ever since I said those hurtful words.

"The box is old, real old," Mr. Potter said.

"How old? Does it say anything about a treasure? Have you ever heard of this Pardonner person? Was he rich?" I asked.

Mr. Potter gave me a strange look. I turned the chest over and showed him the writing on the bottom.

"French, early French for sure," Mr. Potter said. He quickly added, "I think I can help you solve the mystery of this Pardonner fellow."

I could hardly wait. I knew, just knew, that this was the jackpot, the treasure we'd been searching for. I started to imagine all the crazy stories about a rich French explorer, a famous Frenchman.

"Pardonner isn't a man's name, but it is a French word," Mr. Potter said.

"If it's not a person's name, then what does it mean? Riches? Gold? Silver?"

Mr. Potter shook his head.

"It doesn't mean any of those things, boys. Pardonner is the French word for forgive."

~ 32 ~

The words hit me like a ton of bricks smashing down. I looked at T.J. who had his head down. Right away I knew what I had to do. Mr. Potter's words just reinforced it.

"Hey, T.J., I'm sorry for what I said to you by the river. I didn't mean it," I said.

Instantly, I felt a huge relief. It felt like a heavy weight was lifted off my back. I felt free. Dad was right; it's much easier to forgive than to carry hate. T.J. felt it too.

"Thanks, I really appreciate it." Then he added, "I'm sorry for a lot of things too."

I knew what he meant. Even though he had a lot of material things, T.J. didn't have many friends, and we had been more like enemies than family. He needed us, and in a strange way, Kyle and I needed a relationship with him too.

"Let's all hug," Kyle joked.

Everyone laughed, but change was in the air. The hurt and bad feelings that had been built up over the years seemed to disappear, all because of three words, "I am sorry." I was amazed at how free I felt after saying those words. Things were going to be different for the three of us. Things were going to be better.

"Well, boys. I hate to interrupt your family reunion but time is moving on. Let's call Mr. Wilson, the janitor, down to break into this chest," Mr. Potter said.

I looked at Kyle, and he smiled.

"No need. We have the key," Kyle said with a grin.

Mr. Potter looked puzzled. I threw the chest in my backpack, and the three of us went out together. Leaving Mr. Potter's class had a very different feeling. We had left that class together so many times, the three of us. It was different this time. For the first time in our life we left like a family.

Later that day on the bus, we sat with T.J.

Everyone stared. No one could believe that we were all getting along so well.

The bus ride took about an hour, and in that time, we really got to know T.J a lot better. Since junior high I hadn't talked to him about his life or what he liked. It turns out, he's a pretty cool kid. He loves hunting just like we do.

One thing was for sure, Uncle Tom was almost as hard to live with as he was to talk to. T.J. told us how his dad was never happy, and how he always felt pressure to be the best and have the best. T.J. was raised never to be satisfied.

"It's hard to be a Titus. I try, but sometimes I don't think I can ever make my dad happy," T.J. said and added, "I know one thing: money can't buy you happiness."

That we all knew. We didn't need to speak about it again. All the money and material things T.J. had didn't seem so attractive any more. I was glad my dad wasn't like that. I was proud my dad worked at the hardware store every day.

When we reached our bus stop, T.J. turned to me and said, "I'm sorry my dad and I tried to steal your treasure."

Kyle and I got out of our seat. I stopped and turned back to T.J.

"Come on, T.J. You're getting off at our place tonight, at your cousins' house. We've got an important chest to open together."

T.J. jumped up from his seat. The three of us went toward the front of the bus.

As we were going down the aisle, T.J. leaned forward and whispered, "What are we going to tell Mr. Tron? He isn't going to let me off the bus. I don't have a permission note."

I smiled and pointed to Kyle. He was already talking to Mr. Tron when we arrived at the front of the bus.

"You boys are all set. Have a good time at your cousins' house," Mr. Tron said with a wink.

The three of us got off the bus together. T.J. was amazed. He couldn't believe that Mr. Tron had let him off.

"That's Kyle. He can talk anyone into anything," I said.

It was weird. This was the first time T.J. had

been to our house for a long time. Our past problems didn't even matter anymore. What did matter was opening the chest, together, the three of us.

We raced toward the house. Kyle grabbed the spare key that was hidden underneath the front rock by the porch. We knew we had about two hours before Mom and Dad would be home from work.

Kyle and T.J. sat down at the kitchen table, and I headed to our room to retrieve the strange key we'd found by the river. Reaching under my bed, I pulled out the bag that held the artifacts.

I fumbled around for a minute and then felt the outline of the key at the bottom of the bag. I pulled it out of the bag and headed for the kitchen. I turned the corner to see Kyle and T.J. laughing and goofing around—like family, like it's supposed to be.

"You guys ready for this?" I asked.

They both nodded. My mind started to drift as I pictured all the gold coins and money we would have once the treasure chest was open.

My hand was trembling as I put the key in the lock. It fit, but just as it started to turn, I stopped. Seconds went by and both boys looked at me dumbfounded.

"What are you waiting for? Turn the key!" Kyle begged.

"T.J., why don't you open this chest? " I asked.

He smiled. The key turned hard. Dirt and rust fell slowly out of the lock. There was a loud clicking sound, and it sprang open. He took a deep breath and slowly opened the chest. It creaked to life and light shown into it for the first time in over a hundred years.

The real surprise was on us. We couldn't believe our eyes as the chest slowly opened.

~ 33 ~

There was no gold. No silver. In fact, there were only two items. The first was some type of photograph. It didn't look like photos we have now. It was hard to make out, but there were eight men, guys of all ages sitting around a campfire.

They had rifles. It looked like they were ready to go hunting or on some type of adventure. The picture was captivating. Even though it was old and hard to make out, there was something unique about it.

The second item was strange; in fact, it looked like it was made of bones.

"Bones? Maybe they're human," I said.

But they didn't look like human bones.

They were small and connected, forming a longer cone-shaped object. There was a leather strap around them, almost like a necklace. Kyle picked it up and looked around. He wiped it off and slowly put it up to his mouth.

"What are you doing?" I asked.

He smiled and blew into the bony-shaped object. It made a weird sound like Kyle had stepped on a frog. We all laughed.

"It's not human bones; it's a hunting call," Kyle said. "And it's not just any call—it's a turkey call."

We looked at each other astonished. A turkey call! I ran back to our bedroom and came back with a magnifying glass I'd taken out of an old bug kit we'd received for Christmas years earlier. With it I examined the old picture for more clues.

"Well, I'll be!"

Under the magnifying glass, the details in the picture came to life. I could see something laying at the feet of all the men. Turkeys! Not just one or two, but tons of turkeys were piled up. These people were turkey hunters. Around each man's neck was a boned turkey call, just like the one Kyle was holding.

"Let me see that call," I said to Kyle.

He handed it to me, and I felt something on the back. I flipped it over and saw a carving. I took a rag and scrubbed off the dirt and mildew. I could barely make them out, but there were numbers carved into the call that read 15:11.

"Was 15:11 some kind of code or was it stating army time? Maybe it was the date or something," I said.

I started blowing on it and making different sounds, and within minutes I had it sounding like a turkey.

"You know what this means?" I asked.

Kyle and T.J. both looked at me. They couldn't understand why I wasn't acting more disappointed because there was no gold and nothing with any monetary value.

I had found something better. The search for this treasure had led us back to our cousin, and now this turkey call was going to do something I hadn't been able to do. Ever.

I went to the window and looked toward the clouds building on the horizon. A storm was coming. The clouds were big and rolling. There was no doubt in my mind that another violent spring storm was brewing. This storm was going to have high winds, loud thunder, and nasty lightning. I decided right then what we needed to do.

"There's a storm coming. It's time to go hunting!"

"Huh?" T.J. questioned.

"We don't have much time. I'll explain it all once we get to the turkey blind."

- 34 -

We started throwing on our camouflage. Kyle tossed T.J. some of his to put on. I could tell T.J. was confused, but he wasn't asking any questions.

I went to the gun cabinet without thinking, and there sat that old single-shot .16-gauge. It looked magnificent. Someone had fixed the gun. Someone had it ready, ready for the three of us to add that thirteenth slash.

"Why are you taking that old gun?" T.J. asked.

I chuckled. At this point T.J. was probably thinking his newfound family was crazy. I just smiled and grabbed some shells. The three of us took off through the backyard toward the turkey tent by the river.

The closer we got to our hunting blind, the darker the sky grew. The tent was set up just across the river from where T.J. and Uncle Tom had been tearing apart the countryside, the place where we had started looking for the treasure. That didn't matter now.

We could hear thunder in the distance. Kyle quickly set out our two decoys. T.J. was unzipping the tent when he heard him!

GOBBLE! GOBBLE! GOBBLE!

T.J. froze in fear.

"What was that?" he asked, with a trembling voice.

I didn't have time to explain. Scarface was too close. I motioned for T.J. to get into the tent. The three of us sat down. I was on the far left of the blind so the big bird would have to cross in front of me.

All was quiet and then a big boom of thunder roared. The storm was close. The three of us jumped off our camp stools. After the thunder, Scarface let loose with a monstrous gobble of his own. But the sound was softer than his usual one, so we knew the big turkey was moving away from our location.

"Quick, grab the turkey call," I said.

Kyle reached into his backpack and pulled out our treasure, the old wing bone turkey call. I grabbed it, careful not to break it. I slipped the crusty rope around my neck and looked at the other two and smiled.

I blew with all my might, and the call made a beautiful sound. I had used many turkey calls in the past, but none made a sound so sweet. As soon as I hit the call, Scarface thundered back.

GOBBLE! GOBBLE! GOBBLE!

I blew the call again. Instantly, Scarface responded, and this time he was real close. I readied my gun. A slow drizzle started to dance on the tent, and thunder boomed in the distance. Lightning was a couple miles away on the horizon. We didn't have much time.

I saw movement to my left. There was Scarface! He was coming toward the decoys at full strut. He looked even bigger than I remembered. He was so close that I could see his scar, the one that I had given him. I started to shake. Kyle and T.J. were shaking too.

Scarface was standing ten feet away! His presence was amazing! His spring colors seemed to glow as he strutted toward the decoys. His head was a magnificent red, white, and blue.

I could barely breathe. I tried to steady the gun as it bounced around in my hand. I slowly pulled back the hammer, and the gun made a loud clicking noise that instantly caught the attention of the turkey.

The bird stopped and spun, looking right at our tent. His eyes were sharp and piercing, looking right through it. Then Scarface let out the loudest, most ferocious gobble just as a bolt of lightning crashed on the horizon.

I tried to put the small BB sight on his head and pulled the trigger. But instead of hearing a boom, all I heard was a loud click as the hammer crashed forward. The gun didn't go off, but this time it wasn't the gun's fault. In all the excitement, I had forgotten to put a shell in!

~ 35 ~

After all this time, I had screwed up again. Again! I had the bird of my dreams dead in my sights and forgot to load the gun. I put my head down, trying not to cry. Then I heard laughter. I looked up and saw Kyle and T.J. both laughing. My first reaction was anger, but for some reason I started laughing too. I couldn't help it.

"Dude, that was awesome!" T.J. said.

Kyle nodded, "That bird is huge. Kent, that was so cool."

They were right. The whole experience was great—finding the chest, getting T.J. back, and calling in Scarface with an old wing bone turkey call used by the early ancestors of Bellsville. How could I be mad I didn't get that old turkey?

We looked outside the tent and saw that the the once dark sky was now clearing, and birds were out, singing a sweet symphony.

And with that, Scarface was gone, probably forever. Gone with him were his secrets. Where did he live? How did he manage to hide from everyone? Why did he only make an appearance during a storm? I guessed we'd never know.

You don't get too many chances at a bird like that. I'd gotten two, so I thought I was lucky. It also made me realize that most people don't often get a second chance. We now had a chance to bring our family back together again. It started with the three of us.

We walked back to the house talking about our incredible day. There was nothing that could ruin it, not even missing a monster turkey!

We started taking off our hunting stuff on the back porch and walked into our house. As soon as we got through the back door, we stopped. Sitting at the table were Dad and Uncle Tom. They didn't look very happy. In fact, they looked angry. If looks could have killed, the three of us would have died right there in our kitchen.

- 36 -

"T.J.,where have you been?" asked Uncle Tom as he gritted his teeth.

In all the excitement after school, T.J. had forgotten to call home to tell his parents he was at our house.

Dad looked at Kyle and me with that "you're-in-big-trouble" look.

"But Dad. Please listen. We talked, and now things are—" T.J began.

Uncle Tom cut him off.

"Enough! You've done plenty to embarrass me. I don't want to hear another word. I can't believe you're at *their* house!"

I could understand why Uncle Tom would be worried not knowing where T.J. was or if he was safe. But it seemed like he was really mad because T.J. was with us.

"Hold on one second, Tom. What's wrong with our house?" Dad asked quickly.

Both men stood up and stared at each other. They started to argue. I knew I had to do something.

"Just STOP! For once, please listen to us," I yelled.

I pulled out the old picture and threw it on the table. They stopped arguing as I walked over and placed the turkey call and chest on the table in front of them.

"Dad, this is the treasure we were looking for," T.J. said

Uncle Tom picked up the picture and looked at it while Dad started to examine the chest.

"Who is Pardonner?" Dad asked.

"Dad, it's not a person; it's a French word. It means to forgive," Kyle told him.

Both men looked at each other briefly but quickly looked away after making eye contact. I could tell they needed more. They still weren't convinced. We started to tell them the entire story. We even told them about Scarface. We sat for about an hour talking, and when we were done, Uncle Tom stood up.

"Great story, boys. T.J., let's go," said Uncle Tom obviously unmoved by it all.

T.J. stood up and walked toward his dad. All the events of the day weren't an accident. There was a reason everything happened the way it did, a reason we found the chest. There was something much bigger at work in our family than any giant turkey or treasure hunt.

Nevertheless, it still wasn't enough to change Uncle Tom's heart. We needed to give him more.

"There's still one thing about this mystery that we can't understand," Kyle said.

"Does 15:11 mean anything to you?" I asked.

Uncle Tom quickly shook his head.

"It has no meaning to me," he said sharply.

It was obvious that he was feeling uncomfortable and wanted to get out of our house.

"Stay right here," Dad said as he went to the bookshelf in the den. He was an avid reader and had a huge library of books. He came back with a book that was old and had a torn brown cover. I instantly recognized it; it was a book that Dad read everyday.

He opened it and sat down at the table.

"What's this?" Uncle Tom asked.

"Here's your answer, boys," Dad said as he placed the book in the center of the table. I scooted forward and knew the book was Dad's Bible. "Luke 15:11 tells a very important story; it's often referred to as the story of the Prodigal Son."

I'd heard the story many times in Sunday School. In it, a son demands all his inheritance and fortune from his father. Then he takes it and spends it all, wasting it. Now too embarrassed to return home, he feels that what he has done is unforgivable, that there is no way his dad could ever forgive him.

After hitting rock bottom, he decides his one choice is to return and beg for forgiveness. The son was scared that his dad wouldn't be able to forgive him for all the pain he had caused. But not only did the dad forgive his son for everything, he actually ran to him with open arms.

The story was about forgiveness! All this was too real. Dad looked at Uncle Tom and said, "Let's go outside and talk, just you and me."

They headed outside, and we ran to the window and watched as they talked. At first it looked like they were arguing, but they weren't. After several minutes, they shook hands. Something was different, something had changed their hearts. For the first time, I saw my Uncle Tom differently—as an uncle.

I didn't know what was going to happen in the future, but I knew that this adventure hadn't happened by accident. It changed all our lives for the better. They walked into the house laughing.

"Uncle Tom, can T.J. stay at our house tonight?" I asked, hoping it wasn't too soon to ask.

"Of course. That's what families are for," he said with a grin. He added, "Maybe this weekend all of us can go hunting and put another notch in that old gun."

That night we planned on staying up really late, eating junk food and playing video games in our bedroom. It was just getting dark when we heard more thundering in the distance. We went out the back door onto the porch and watched Mother Nature as she lit up the sky with an amazing lightning storm.

We were at peace; we were a family. We sat and admired the storm for a couple minutes without a care in the world. Just as we were about to go inside, T.J. saw something moving.

"I think I just saw something flying around that sign," he said as he pointed to the huge lighted billboard across our property.

"All I see is your dad smiling, waving to his nephews," I said with a grin.

We all laughed and continued staring at the sign. Suddenly I caught movement too, but I couldn't tell what it was.

"Guys, I just saw something too," I said.

Kyle said, "It's probably just a raccoon."

"Yeah, you're probably right," I said.

The three of us went back to talking. After a couple minutes, we decided to head inside. I was the last one but stopped just as I was about to enter.

"Come on, Kent," Kyle called from inside.

I stood there, staring at the lit-up billboard. Something inside, down deep in my gut, was telling me to stop.

"Grab some flashlights. There's still one more treasure that we haven't found," I said.

Kyle went to the junk drawer and pulled out three flashlights, and we set off across the field toward the sign. When we got there, the three of us stood quietly. After about ten minutes of listening and not hearing anything but the sound of crickets, I turned to Kyle and T.J.

"Sorry, guys. I guess old Scarface is still driving me nuts. Let's head back to the house," I said.

With that, the other two went inside. When I got to the door, I took one more look back at the sign. There, roosting as big and strong as ever, stood Scarface. He looked in our direction and let out one of his famous ear-piercing gobbles. With one swift turn, he ducked behind the sign to his secret sanctuary to live another day.

I went over to the gun cabinet and pulled out

that old single-shot. I grabbed a jackknife and headed toward the den so the three of us could scratch notch #13 into the stock.

We'd finally found Scarface's secret and unraveled a couple of our own. And most importantly, we found the treasure of being a whole family once again.

About the Author

Lane Walker is an award-winning author, speaker, and educator. His book collection, Hometown Hunters, won a Bronze Medal at the Moonbeam Awards for Best Kids series.

Lane is an accomplished outdoor writer in Michigan. He has been writing for the past 15 years and has over 250 articles professionally published. Walker has a real passion for hunter recruitment and getting kids in the outdoors. He is a former teacher and current principal living in Michigan with his wife and four kids.

Lane is a highly sought after professional speaker traveling to schools, churches and wild game dinners.

To book Lane for an event or to find out more check out www.lanewalkerbooks.com or contact him at info@lanewalkerbooks.com.